GATOR GIRLZ

STRONG SOUTHERN WOMEN SERIES
BOOK TWO

ALI SPOONER

GATOR GIRLZ

STRONG SOUTHERN WOMEN SERIES
BOOK TWO

ALI SPOONER

Affinity
Rainbow Publications

2018

ACKNOWLEDGMENTS

I would like to thank my fans for following my stories, providing great feedback and encouragement. Writing wouldn't be so much fun without you. Thanks to Affinity, Irish Dragon for the cover art and the team of editors, readers, and publishers who continue to help me grow as a writer.

DEDICATION

This story is for Haeden, and Emily. I hope you grow up together to be as close as Cam and Sandy. Love you both!

TABLE OF CONTENTS

CHAPTER ONE

When Cam St. Angelo and Tab Fortner returned to Baton Rouge after the NCAA Softball tournament in Oklahoma City, it was time to say goodbye to their friends and teammates for the summer. They would see each other again in mid-June, and then in mid-July for a weeklong softball camp. Cam had received confirmation from her coach, that Wanda, Cam's thirteen-year-old sister, and Logan, Wanda's best friend and teen crush, had slots reserved for the July camp. She planned to share the news with them when she returned home for the summer. Just as Cam had promised, she and Tab would share a weekend with Wanda and Logan, at the hunt camp on The Island, to give them an opportunity to discover their feelings for one another.

"I'll see you in two weeks for the campout, right?" Cam asked Tab.

"If not before. I don't cherish the thought of spending this summer with my mother."

Cam could hear the sadness in her voice. She wrapped her lover in her arms. "We'll put you to work, but you're more than welcome to spend as much time as you can with my family. We can take over the hunt camp for the summer, and I'll teach you how to be a country girl."

"Are you serious?"

"Absolutely. You're a part of our family now and are welcome any time."

"Do you need to clear that with your folks?"

Cam gave her a sweet smile. "It's already cleared. It was Dad's suggestion."

"No way."

"Yes way. He knows how happy you make me. He will work you hard, though."

"I'm not afraid of hard work. I'd do anything to be able to spend the summer with y'all."

"I'll go ahead and move out to the hunt camp, then. That way my sister Teresa doesn't have to bunk with the others again. And at seventeen, I'm sure she'll appreciate that. We'll have some privacy that way too. You know Mini-Me will insist on spending time with us, though."

Tab chuckled. "Sandy is such a sweetheart. I don't mind sharing you with her at all."

"Oh no, my dear, it's you she'll want to spend time with. I hope you like to fish."

Tab blushed with a confession. "Um, I've never been fishing."

Cam stepped back to look at her. "Never, ever?"

"Nope, so you'll have to teach me."

"You will have two of the best teachers ever."

"That sounds like fun. What kind of clothes do I need to bring?"

"Jeans, shorts, T-shirts, some work boots if you have them. If not, you can use a pair of mine."

"I'll be borrowing a pair. The closest thing I have is hiking boots."

"Those wouldn't be bad to bring."

"Would it be okay if I come down next weekend?"

"That would be perfect."

They kissed, and when Cam stepped back, she said, "Let's go say goodbye to Liz and Ruth." Liz and Ruth were their teammates and best friends, and Cam was really going to miss them.

†

After agreeing to meet Ruth and Liz back on campus a week before the first camp, Tab and Cam started for home.

"I love you," Tab said as they walked to their vehicles. "I'll call you soon."

"Love you too. Can't wait to see you next weekend. Drive carefully."

She watched Tab's Mustang disappear, then drove by the stadium on her way off campus. Cam smiled as she thought about her freshman year. She had survived her first year of classes and found she really enjoyed college life. Living away from home had given her experiences that had made her mature and realize she was rapidly becoming a leader. It was different from being with her sisters, and her desire to be the best had made a lasting impression not only with her teammates, but within the friendships she had developed. While she hadn't realized her dream of playing in the national softball tournament, she had experienced a great first year. The disappointment of losing in the Super Regionals charged her motivation and desire to work harder in the coming year. Most importantly, she had found love. Cam had never dreamed that falling in love could feel the way Tab made her feel. The smile grew on her face with every passing mile. The year had been great, but she was ready to be home.

†

Cam pulled up to find Sandy, her baby sister, and her dad, Ronny, sitting on the porch waiting for her arrival. Sandy bolted off the porch and ran to meet her big sister.

"Hey, Squirt," Cam said as she climbed down from her Jeep. She picked Sandy up and twirled her. She was amazed at how much her nine-year-old sister had grown.

"I am so glad you are home," she squealed as Cam spun her around.

"Me too, and I have a surprise for you." She placed Sandy back on the ground.

"What is it?"

"Tab is going to be spending some of the summer with us, and I need you to teach her how to fish."

Sandy looked at her, and lifted her hand to block the sun from her eyes. She scrunched up her nose. "She doesn't know how to fish?"

"Did you forget Tab's a city girl?"

"Yeah, I guess I did. I can teach her. That'll be fun."

"I figured you were just the person for the job."

Her dad had walked up. "So Tab's going to join us for the summer?"

"Part of it anyhow. We've got a couple softball camps to host, but she'll be down this weekend."

"That's great news. Your mama and sisters have cleaned the hunt camp for you this week and stocked it with some basic supplies. You'll still come home for meals, right?"

"Oh, heck yeah," Cam answered.

Sandy took a bag Cam handed her. "Mama's making your favorite meal to welcome you home: fried chicken, cream corn, with rice and gravy."

"Now we're talking." Cam grinned. "Will you help me carry these out to the boat?"

"We both will." Her dad took two bags from her. "Lunch should be ready soon."

Cam grabbed the last of her bags, and they carried them to the dock and placed them in one of the aluminum boats. "You want to go out with me later to get set up at the camp?"

"Can I spend the night out there with you tonight?" Sandy asked.

"If Mama approves, then yes you can."

As they walked back to the house, Cam slipped her arm around her dad's shoulder. "What are we doing tomorrow?"

"Sleeping in. It's Sunday and your mama has convinced me to take the day off when we can. We can get back after it Monday. We've got cane to cut for mash, and some summer corn ready to be picked and taken to market."

"Since we'll be staying out at the camp this summer, I'll need to tell Tab about cooking the moonshine. Is that okay with you?"

"Do you have any worries about telling her?"

"No, I can explain everything to her just fine."

"I've got no problem, then. I trust your judgment."

Cam patted his shoulder. "Thanks, Dad."

"Has she really never been fishing?"

She chuckled. "Never, ever."

"Tony at LB's told me he'd take as many catfish as we can bring him this summer. That sounds like the perfect job for the three of y'all." LB's was the local processing plant for gator hides and other food sources obtained from the bayou.

Sandy looked up at him. "He's going to skin them, right?"

Ronny laughed softly. "Yes, honey, he'll have his boys process them. You just catch and deliver them."

Sandy turned her gaze to her sister. "Can we start tomorrow, Cam?"

Cam looked at her dad, who nodded. "It's up to you."

"Sure thing, Squirt. Not at the crack of dawn, though."

Her dad grinned. "You can come over for breakfast and then load up your gear."

†

Wanda met them at the back door. "Mama's got lunch on the table."

"I reckon we better come in and eat then." Ronny winked at Cam.

Cam held the door for everyone. "It sure smells good in here, Mama," she said as she walked into the dining room and hugged her.

"Welcome home, Cam."

"Thanks for cooking all this. It's quite a spread."

"Come eat it while it's hot."

The family shared a feast together. Cam told them about the playoffs and her experiences with Tab at the national tournament. When she mentioned Tab's broken arm, Sandy frowned.

"Is Tab going to be okay?" Sandy asked.

"Yes, she's healing well and will be out of the cast soon," Cam assured her.

"Will she be able to fish?"

"Yeah, Squirt, she will."

Camille refilled Cam's tea glass. "I'm glad Tab's going to be able to spend the summer with us, or at least part of it."

"She was delighted with the invitation." Cam frowned. "Her parents aren't the warmest people I've ever met. Let me correct that—her dad was cool, but her mother is a snob. Tab wasn't looking forward to spending the summer with her."

Camille shook her head. "That's no way to treat your child. I hope she'll feel welcome here."

"I've no doubt she will, Mama. She loves it here, says it feels like a home to her."

"She can come out anytime she wants. I hope she knows that."

Cam scooped up a final bite of rice and gravy. "If she doesn't know already, she will soon. Squirt is going to teach her to fish."

Wanda dropped her fork. "She doesn't know how to fish?"

"She's a city girl," Sandy reminded her. "I'm going to fix that."

Ronny chuckled and looked at Cam. "You think Tab has any idea what she's getting into?"

"Probably not, but she adjusts really well."

"Sandy told me she's going to stay at the camp with you tonight. You want me to pack up some of these leftovers to send with ya?" Camille asked.

Cam grinned. "That would be perfect."

"Let's get you set for dinner, and your sisters can clean up the kitchen for me."

"I can help," Cam insisted.

"I know, but you need to go get settled into the camp. You sure you'll be okay staying out there?"

"Yes, but I'll take my pistol with me if it'll make you feel better."

Sandy scowled at Camille. "Why, Mama?"

"In case she runs into a snake or something."

"Oh, okay."

†

Sandy carried a pitcher of sweet tea, and Cam brought two large plates of food to the boat. Sandy untied the lines as Cam secured the food, and they drove across the bayou to the hunt camp. The sun was starting to fade as they finished unloading the boat, and Cam settled into the camp. The small two-bedroom cabin was perfect for a summer getaway and would still give her the freedom she'd become accustomed to at college. She was thankful her parents realized how much more independent she had become while away from home.

"The only thing about being out here is there's no TV," Sandy complained.

"I can live without television. It's all reruns in the summer anyhow, and we'll be too busy to be bored."

"I'm so glad I get to teach Tab how to fish."

"She's going to love it. Fishing will be a good opportunity for you to earn some money this summer. Speaking of this summer, you've got a birthday coming up. Any ideas of what you want?"

"Naw, not really."

"I saw Mama brought out several of her jigsaw puzzles. Are you up for working on one?"

"That sounds like fun. You want me to grab us something to drink?"

"You can bring me a beer, and I'll get the puzzle out on the table."

Cam opened her beer after Sandy brought it, and they were scattering the puzzle pieces on the table when her phone rang. She looked at the screen and saw Tab's number. "Keep going. I'll be back in a few."

Sandy rolled her eyes and grinned. "It must be Tab," she teased.

"Yeah, it is, smarty pants." Cam answered the phone. "Hey there," she said as she walked into the bedroom. "Yeah, I'm all settled in at the camp. Sandy and me are going to work on a jigsaw puzzle." Cam sat on the bed. "I wish you were here too, sweetie." She sighed. "I'm sorry your mom's not happy with you, but the family is so ready for you to be here. Sandy's excited to teach you to fish, and one of the local companies will buy as many fish as y'all can catch." She listened to Tab for several minutes. "Sandy was asking when you'd get your cast off. I'm glad you have an appointment Monday." She chuckled. "I bet you are ready to get it off, but you'll still need to be careful for a while."

She smiled. "We're going fishing tomorrow, but not until after breakfast. Yes, I'll tell them all hello for you. I miss you too, baby. I'm looking forward to seeing you next week. That works for me. Get here as soon as you can. Yes, call me tomorrow. Love you too."

They had been apart less than a day, but Cam was missing Tab already. Hopefully she'd stay busy until Tab got here, so she wouldn't dwell on their separation. She plugged her phone into the charger and placed it beside the bed. Her pistol was lying there, and she hoped she would have no need to use it over the summer.

When she walked back into the kitchen, Sandy was kneeling in a chair, busily turning the puzzle pieces faceup.

"Well, darn, I thought you'd have it done by now."

Sandy looked up at her. "You're such a goof. When's Tab coming down?"

"Later in the week. She's excited you're gonna be teaching her to fish."

"I'm looking forward to it too. I can't believe she doesn't know how to fish."

"I imagine there are a few things we'll be teaching her this summer." Cam sat next to Sandy and rubbed her hands together. "This is going to be fun."

†

After a hearty breakfast, Wanda walked with them out to the boat. Cam sent Sandy into the workshop to get a bucket of bait, then turned to Wanda. "Do you still want to invite Logan out to the hunt camp?"

"Yes, I do. She's excited to meet the famous Cam St. Angelo, and her girlfriend."

"Ha! I'm nowhere near famous."

"Not according to Coach. She constantly raves about you. You're a celebrity at school, even if you don't believe it."

"Whatever." Cam chuckled. "Tab will be down this weekend, so how about next weekend?"

"Do we need to check with Dad about his schedule?"

"That's not a bad idea. I'll leave that up to you, and you can fill me in later, okay?"

"I will. Thanks, Cam."

She pulled Wanda into a hug. "You're welcome. I'm looking forward to meeting Logan."

Sandy returned with the bait and climbed straight into the boat. "All set, Cam."

"Will you untie us and toss the mooring line to Squirt?"

Wanda smiled. "You got it."

"Let's get some fish." Cam grinned as she started the motor.

†

Three hours later, Sandy had filled the live well with fish.

"Should we swing by LB's to see if anyone is working today?" Sandy grinned at Cam, excited with the day's catch.

Cam nodded. "It can't hurt."

Cam increased pressure on the throttle as they headed across the water toward town. As they approached the docks, Cam noticed the movement of workers at LB's.

"Looks like we're in luck." She waved when Tony Doucet stepped out onto the dock. "Toss him the line, Squirt."

Cam slowed the boat, allowing it to coast toward the dock. Tony caught the line and guided them into a slip.

"Whatcha got there, Squirt?"

"Our first delivery of catfish," she answered.

"Let's check them out. Let me grab a tub."

Sandy threw open the cover to reveal the fish she had caught and smiled when Tony stepped into the boat. "Whoa der, you been busy, little one. You catch all these cats by yourself?"

"Sho nuff did," she answered.

Tony looked at Cam, who had stretched out at the console. She nodded. "Every single one of them. I'm just the driver."

She watched as they placed the fish in the tub.

"Wow, dey be heavy too. Did you stuff 'em with rocks?"

Sandy chuckled. "No, Mr. Tony. Just big, fat, fish."

"These are perfect for filets. Keep 'em coming."

"Cam says we can fish every day after we finish our chores."

"Let's go weigh these and see what you've got."

Cam took one handle on the side of the tub and helped him carry it from the boat to the scales. They put it on one, and Tony subtracted the weight of the tub. "Eighty-seven pounds. That's a great catch."

Cam turned and gave Sandy a high five. "Way to go, Squirt."

Tony hit a button on a small adding machine to print off a receipt. He logged in her catch. "You okay with a weekly payment?"

Sandy looked at Cam, who nodded to her. "That sounds good to me, Mr. Tony." Sandy held her hand out and they shook. "Deal."

"I've entered this on the books but keep the receipt for your record. I bet Cam will have a Ziploc you can put them in until I give you a check this Friday."

"See you tomorrow then," Sandy said.

"Thanks, Tony," Cam said as they climbed back into the boat.

†

"Eighty-seven pounds!" Ronny was in disbelief. "That's a lot of fish."

"She filled up the live well," Cam said.

Ronny's chest puffed out with pride. "Take the bigger boat home with you tomorrow. It's got a deeper live well."

Cam nodded to her dad. "You may hit a hundred pounds with the extra space, Sandy. You think there's a danger of running out of catfish, Dad?"

"The way Sandy is catching them we may run out this summer."

"No way, Dad," Sandy replied.

"Maybe not, but you may need to change fishing holes every now and then so you don't overfish an area."

"We can head out to the far side of the island tomorrow and start working our way back," Cam told her. "Better get a good night's sleep. I think we have to harvest mudbugs tomorrow before we can fish. Is that right?" She looked at her father.

"Yes, it is. Do you want us to pick you up at the camp in the morning?" he asked.

13

"Why don't we run two boats tomorrow? Sandy can help you, and Wanda can run with me." Sandy opened her mouth to protest. "That way we'll have all afternoon to fish."

"That's a good idea. We got mash ready to cook for Tuesday night. Are you up for helping me?"

"Sure, Dad, I'll get Sandy and Wanda to help me load some buckets for the mudbugs, and then I'll head back to camp and see you in the morning."

"I'll send some ham biscuits out with Wanda," her mama called from the kitchen.

"Let's do it, then." Cam took her two youngest sisters out to the workshop for buckets to place in both boats.

†

Cam drove across the bayou as the sun drifted below the horizon. The last rays faded from the water as she pulled into the canal at the hunt camp. She tied off the boat and climbed onto the dock. The crickets and nighttime symphony began as she walked toward the camp.

I think it's time for a beer and some relaxing. She pulled out a cold beer and took a seat at the dining room table, smiling at the jigsaw puzzle she and Sandy had started. Her gaze drifted across the pieces, and she picked out one and found its mate. Cam grinned as she remembered spooning with Tab. Snuggling into her body felt like puzzle pieces sliding into place. She looked at the clock and decided it would be too early to call Tab. Her family tended to eat dinner a bit later, so she would sip on her beer and allow working on the puzzle to relax her. Piece after piece fell into place as Cam's beer sat untouched.

The deep croaking of a bull gator broke the silence.

"Damn, that sounds close." Cam walked to her room and grabbed her pistol before stepping out onto the back porch with a flashlight. The croaking continued as she walked outside, the sound vibrating across the heavy air. She searched the backyard and found it empty, and she aimed the flashlight toward the banks of the canal. The beam caught bright eyes as the gator let out a low rumbling growl. The hair on the back of her neck rose.

"You're a big sumbitch, but you better hope Bubba Gump doesn't find you in his territory." She had barely spoken the words when another gator croaked in the distance. "Right on cue, Bubba."

Cam had never seen two bull gators do battle, but she had witnessed the aftermath of Bubba Gump defending his territory. On numerous occasions, she had run across mutilated gator carcasses, evidence that Bubba did not tolerate another large male in his domain.

The gator slid into the water and disappeared from her view.

The crickets and frogs resumed their chorus, and Cam returned inside. She placed her pistol on the table, picked up her warm beer, and took a sip.

"Yuck," Cam cursed and poured the remainder down the drain. She settled back into her puzzle until her phone rang. Cam looked at Tab's number on the screen and smiled as she answered.

"Hey there." Her smile grew when she heard Tab's voice. "I miss you too. I can't wait for you to get here, either. Your fishing teacher is excited as well." She listened to Tab for a few minutes as she told her about the boring weekend she'd have at her parents' house. "You know you can come earlier. We've got lots of things planned for you."

She thought her face would crack when Tab told her she'd be there Wednesday. "That's great news, baby. Maybe I can survive three more days." Cam toyed with a puzzle piece. "I was just messing around with a jigsaw puzzle Sandy and I started. I'm going to shower and get ready for bed soon. Tomorrow's going to be a busy day. … Yes, I'll call you when I'm ready for bed. Okay, I'll talk to you soon."

Cam ended the call, still smiling at the purr in Tab's voice.

†

Cam locked the door to the cabin and walked into the bedroom. She turned on the shower before stripping and plugged her phone in to charge. The tepid water felt wonderful as it washed away the grime from the day's hard work. It was great to be home, and her parents' suggestion that she spend the summer in the hunt camp was working out perfectly. She saw her family daily but had privacy as well. A short boat ride would bring her back to the Island after working or visiting with her family. Tab would be here soon, and they could create some special memories of their own.

She wanted to share so much with Tab; her life working alongside her family was a huge part of who she was. Cam was excited that Tab was genuinely eager to spend most of the summer with them, instead of with her parents.

After bathing, she rinsed and dried herself before climbing into bed. She had lit a candle, reminding her of Tab, and the soft fragrance wafted through the room as the shadows danced on the walls and ceiling. With a smile plastered to her face, she punched the favorites listing for Tab's number.

†

Tab had excused herself from the dinner table and gone upstairs to shower. Her mother's endless complaints about her current case were beginning to drive her insane. Her father had become expert in blocking out her voice but Tab had yet to learn that skill. When her mother had made a sarcastic remark about Tab traveling to the boondocks to stay with Cam and her family, Tab's patience had reached its limit. Her teeth clenched as she thought up a semi-polite response, and her father winked at her for showing restraint. He clearly knew Tab wanted to blast her mother's snootiness right back at her.

Tab locked her door behind her and took a leisurely shower, washing away the venom of her mother's words. No matter what her mother felt or said about Cam, Tab was certain she loved her girlfriend. Tab didn't give a damn about her mother's lectures on social status. Cam's family wasn't rich by any stretch of the imagination, their love for each other was worth more than any amount of money could buy. Tab would gladly trade the big house and her fast car for a mere morsel of the love the St. Angelos shared.

She dried and slipped between freshly laundered sheets as she waited for Cam to call.

†

"Hey, darling," Cam said when Tab answered. When Tab spoke, she sounded tense. "Is your mother giving you a hard time? … Yes, I can hear it in your voice."

Cam listened as Tab described her miserable evening, allowing her to purge the for a short napfor you to do here." Tab chuckled softly.

"Yes, I'm all alone." Tab asked her to place her phone on speaker next to her on the bed. "Are you feeling a bit naughty tonight?" she asked Tab. "Yes, I know. I can't wait for you to be beside me, either."

Tab's voice changed to a soft, sexy purr and moisture spread between Cam's legs.

"Okay, yes, I'm listening."

As Tab described what she'd like to be doing to Cam's body, Cam gently stroked her belly. She closed her eyes and imagined Tab lying beside her as Tab's hands toyed with her nipples and grazed her lips down Cam's neck. "Uhmm, yes, that feels great. Yes, my nipples are hard just waiting for your lips." Her nipples had pebbled with excitement as Cam gently tugged and twisted them. She imagined Tab's warm mouth sucking them, teeth gently nibbling the tips as Tab's hand glided down the front of her body. Her fingers reached her damp curls. "You have me so wet, Tab. … No, I'm not inside yet. Oh yes, I want to come with you, baby. I want to slide my tongue deep inside your wetness and stroke you from the bottom all the way to your clit."

Cam had never experienced phone sex before, but she could easily imagine her lover touching and teasing her. Moisture seeped from her lips as her fingertips followed the path of Tab's voice. She trembled with anticipation as Tab's words filled the room, her voice quivering with emotion as they made love through their touch and words.

"I need to go inside soon, Tab." Her voice was a breathy whisper. Tab's breathing sped, and she knew her lover was eager for release as well. "You've got me so wet, my fingers slid in so easily. Feels good Tab, don't stop."

Cam slid her fingers inside herself, and they were welcomed by the velvety wetness and the throbbing deep inside her walls. She expertly teased herself until she was on the verge of orgasm.

Her voice was raspy with need. "I'm not sure I can hold on much longer." Tab's voice was deep with emotion when she answered. "Oh yes, I'm coming with you, Tab," Cam cried as she erupted with an intense orgasm.

Cam didn't regain control of her breathing for several minutes, and judging by the sounds coming across the phone, she assumed Tab was having similar difficulty. "Wow, that was intense and felt so good, Tab."

Tab chuckled softly.

"What's so funny?"

"I can't wait another three days to feel that in person, Cam. I'll be down tomorrow, if that's still okay."

"It will be perfect. Call me when you're getting close and I'll make sure to come meet you."

"That's okay, I can hang with your mama for a bit if you need to finish up working."

"We'll see what time it is. Sandy and I are fishing tomorrow afternoon after we help Dad harvest the mudbugs. She's got a new job, supplying catfish to a local buyer. She caught eighty-seven pounds today."

"That's a lot of fish."

"Dad's swapping boats with me tomorrow so we can use the larger boat with a bigger live well in it for fishing. If it's not too late in the day, your fishing teacher may want to go ahead and begin your lessons."

Tab laughed softly again.

"She's really excited to be teaching you to fish."

"I can't wait. I'll leave after my doctor's appointment and try to be there by one. Will that be a good time for y'all?"

"We should be back from delivering the mudbugs and eating lunch then."

"That sounds really good. If I get there earlier, I can help your mama cook."

"She'll probably shoo you out of the kitchen, but you can sit and talk with her."

"That I can do with no problem. I can't wait to see you."

"Me either. Hopefully tomorrow will pass quickly and you'll be here."

"I love you, Cam."

"I love you too. I bet I sleep like a rock tonight."

"Me too, and we'll have the real thing tomorrow night."

"Yes, we will." Cam remembered agreeing to help her dad cook up a batch of mash Tuesday night. She would need to have a talk with Tab before that happened, but that could wait until she arrived.

"I know you have to get up early in the morning, so I'll wish you sweet dreams, my love."

"You too, Tab. Drive safe tomorrow and I'll see you soon."

†

Cam ended the call and watched the shadows dance for a few minutes until her eyes grew heavy. She blew out the candle and hugged a pillow close before drifting into a deep, peaceful sleep.

CHAPTER TWO

Cam was already dressed and laying a campfire when her dad and two younger sisters pulled up in the larger boat.

"Good morning," she called as they drifted toward the dock. Wanda stepped out of the boat and tied them off.

"It's going to be another beautiful day on the bayou," Ronny said as he joined them.

"Yes, it is. Tab's driving down today, too, so you can start fishing lessons if she gets here in time," she told Sandy.

"Awesome," Sandy cried and slapped her hand in a high five.

"Did you call your mama to tell her to keep an eye open? She and the others are picking corn this morning."

"No, but I will. Let me step back inside for my pistol and I'll be right back."

"Let's swap gear on the boats while we wait on Cam," he told Sandy and Wanda as she walked back into the cabin.

Cam stepped into the bedroom, placed the holstered pistol on her belt, and called her mama to let her know about Tab's early arrival. Her mother was tickled Tab was coming down and would be sure to have extra sandwiches ready for lunch. When Cam returned to the dock, Wanda handed her a plate of biscuits and a thermos of coffee.

Ronny smiled up at Cam. "Change of partners," he said. "Do you and Sandy want to take the northern lines and check out a fishing spot, while Wanda and I run the southern lines?"

"That sounds like a good plan to me." Cam took a bite of the salty ham biscuit. "Do we want to meet back here or over at LB's?"

"We'll just meet you at LB's."

"We'll see you around lunch, then," Cam said as she stepped onto the larger boat and secured her food and coffee at the console. "Let's go get us some mudbugs." She grinned at Sandy, who was untying their line.

"Just waiting on you, boss." She laughed.

Cam started the motor and turned the boat toward open water after Sandy climbed in. They would begin checking lines at their northernmost boundary and work back toward camp. They had a dozen five-gallon buckets to fill, so it should take most of the morning. After delivering them to LB's and going home for lunch, they would pick up Tab and go fishing.

Cam munched on a biscuit as she drove them to their first line. Sandy sat toward the front of the boat and looked out across the open water. Her sandy-blond hair blew across her shoulders in the crisp morning breeze. Cam knew it wouldn't be cool for long as the summer sun began beating down on them.

†

Cam finished a second biscuit as she pulled up to their first trap. She saw the bright pink ribbon attached to the tether line and guided the boat straight toward it. She cut the motor and coasted toward the bank.

"You want to get this one, Squirt?" she asked as the boat came to a halt.

"Sure."

The trap would be heavy if it was full, but Cam had confidence Sandy could pull it up to the side of the boat. "Make ya a deal. You haul 'em up, I'll empty them and bait 'em, and you can put 'em back in the water. Sound good to you?"

"Yup, sounds good to me." Sandy leaned over to grab the line.

"Careful you don't pull anything else up besides the trap."

"Yes, Mama," Sandy tossed back with a grin.

Cam took the trap from her, filled the first bucket nearly to the brim, and dipped a smaller bucket full of water to pour on top to keep them from drying out. She dropped a frozen fish head in the trap and handed it to Sandy.

"You know I was thinking something," Cam said. "Logan and Wanda will be attending the second softball camp this summer. Do you think you should give the fish a week to hide and come up to camp with them? I'm sure we could use a good ball girl."

"I'd love to do that. Do you really think it'd be all right?"

"I'll clear it with Coach, and then Mama and Dad, but I don't see why not. You can stay in the apartment with Tab and me."

"That would be fun," Sandy said as she turned back to her. "That's in July, right?"

"Yep, right after your birthday."

"You'll be home for that, right?"

"I wouldn't miss it for anything."

"Will Tab be here too?"

"Yeah, I would think so."

"Good." Sandy took her seat, ready to move to the next trap.

†

After filling half the buckets, Cam decided they would take a break to eat another biscuit and drink some water.

"Are you looking forward to fishing later?" Cam asked.

"Yeah, I think we should start close to our first trap. I haven't fished there in a long time."

"There's probably some granddaddies there, then."

Sandy lifted a hand to ward the sun from her eyes. "Do you really think we'll hit a hundred pounds today?"

"I wouldn't be surprised." Cam took two hats out of the console and handed one to her. "Here, this should help."

"Thanks." Sandy pulled the hat down on her head.

"Especially if Tab has beginner's luck and starts to catch fish right off the bat."

"Are you going to fish with us too?"

"Yes, if you'd like that. I think there's plenty room for three to fish."

"We could finish faster that way." Sandy grinned.

"Good point. Did you grab bait or do we need to get it when we go in for lunch?"

"When we go in. I didn't think we wanted to smell it all day."

"Another smart move. How did you grow up so fast? When I left for college, you were my baby sister, but you've really grown up this last year."

"Dad has given me more chores with you being away at college. It's helped me to learn all kinds of new things."

"I see that. I'm proud of ya, Squirt."

"Thanks, Cam."

Cam watched her for several minutes while they ate a snack. Not only had Sandy grown several inches, she had matured in other ways.

†

Cam had just emptied the last of their string of traps and handed it to Sandy when her phone rang. She answered the call from Tab. "Really, you're almost here? You must have gotten up early. … Yes, we just emptied our last trap and are almost ready to go drop them." She listened to Tab for several seconds. "I'm glad you're here too. Mama has plenty of help making lunch if you want to ride to LB's with Sandy and me to drop off our catch. … Okay, we'll see you when we get home, then. Be safe. Bye."

She ended the call and grinned at Sandy. "Let's roll."

They started across the open water and met up with Wanda and their dad, as they had also finished their harvest.

Ronny slowed his boat and let Cam take the lead as they drove into town.

†

Bren, Cam's childhood friend and first crush, looked up from her desk when she heard a boat approaching. She smiled when she saw Cam and Sandy in the first boat, and Ronny and Wanda closely following them. She saved the file she was working on and walked downstairs to greet her old friends. The sweltering, humid summer morning bathed her as soon as she stepped out of the air-conditioning. She had to admit to getting spoiled working inside.

Bren started across the concrete platform toward the loading docks and took advantage of the girls tying off the boats to watch Cam work. She had barely seen Cam since she went away to college, but Cam looked fantastic. She was lean, tanned, and Bren thought she had grown an inch or so. When Cam looked up to see her approaching, Bren's heart jumped when they locked eyes and Cam returned her smile.

She lifted her hand in a wave. "Hey, stranger."

"Hey, Bren, how are ya?"

"Doing good, thanks, and y'all?"

"Fantastic. Dropping off some mudbugs and we'll be back later with some cats too."

"Awesome, so I'll be seeing you often this summer?"

"At least for a bit. I've got a couple of softball camps to attend, but we'll be spending a lot of time on the water while I'm home."

Cam handed the last of the buckets over to Tony and stepped onto the dock to hug Bren. "How are you and Rudy doing? No baby yet?"

"Not for a lack of trying, but no, not yet." She grinned. "How are you and Tab doing?"

Cam's face lit up. "Doing great. She's probably at the house now. Hopefully she'll be spending most of the summer with me out at the camp. Sandy's going to teach her how to fish."

"From the look at the fish Sandy's been bringing in, she'll have a great teacher."

Sandy perked up. "Fish fear me," she teased.

Cam smiled at her baby sister. "You got that right, Squirt."

Ronny and Wanda had finished making their delivery and he asked Cam, "You ready for some lunch?"

"I could eat." She grinned back at him. "See you later today, Bren."

"Y'all stay safe and bring us a load of cats," she told Sandy.

"Will do," Sandy called back and untied the line before stepping onto the boat.

†

Camille and Tab were placing plates of sandwiches and bags of chips on the table when Cam and the others arrived. Cam walked over and hugged Tab. "I'm so glad you're here."

"Me too. I can't wait to learn how to fish."

"We'll head out after we have some lunch."

†

Sandy ran ahead of them to retrieve the bucket of smelly bait and then joined them in the boat as Cam asked,

"Are you sure you don't want some sunscreen? The sun is much different out on the water."

"No, I might get a little burned, but if I'm going to be working with y'all this summer, I guess I'd better get used to it."

"Okay, don't say I didn't warn ya." Cam grinned.

She started the motor and they pulled out across the open water. Cam was in heaven, with her two favorite ladies on the boat with her. Tab sat with Sandy at the head of the boat, and she watched Sandy talking animatedly with Tab, probably explaining the wonderful world of fishing. The smile grew on her face as Tab pulled her hair back and slipped her ball cap on her head to keep it out of her face.

Yeah, life doesn't get much better than this.

Cam turned off the motor and let the boat coast into the head of a slough before dropping a small anchor. "It's time to learn how to fish." She beamed at Tab.

Sandy handed Tab a rod and demonstrated how to bait the hook and cast across the water. Tab followed her instructions and cast her line on the opposite side of the boat from Sandy.

"Nice cast," Sandy said, and Tab grinned back at her.

"Now very slowly, start reeling your line in, and if you feel a tug, jerk your line to set the hook. Once you've got it hooked, you crank your reel like crazy until you get him to the boat and we'll net him for you," Sandy explained.

"Oh, oh, I think I'm getting a bite," Tab cried.

"Hold on until you feel a big tug, then hook 'em," Sandy replied.

The end of Tab's rod bowed. "Now," Sandy said.

Tab jerked it to the side and squealed with laughter as she turned the crank on the reel.

Sandy also set her hook and began cranking in a race to see who landed first. Cam picked up the net and moved to the center of the boat to wait.

"Oh, she's got a good one, Sandy," Cam said as Tab concentrated on catching the fish.

"I do too," Sandy answered through gritted teeth. "There's definitely some granddaddies out here."

Cam watched Tab's face when the fish came to the surface again. The look on her face was quickly followed by an exclamation of surprise. "Oh my gosh, he is big," she called out.

"Bring him on in and I'll net him for you," Cam said.

When the heavy fish was close enough to reach, Cam dropped the net and scooped it up. "Woohoo, at least a six pounder, Sandy." She placed the fish on the floor of the boat and took a pair of pliers out of her back pocket. "Now comes the tricky part."

Tab watched Cam carefully place a booted foot on the fish, then use the pliers to remove the hook from its mouth. "You've got to be careful around the whiskers," Sandy warned. "If they spike you it hurts like crazy."

"She's right, so be careful," Cam said as she handed Tab the hook and dropped the fish into the live well. "One fish down and a bunch more to go. How are you coming over there, Squirt?"

"Get your net ready," she answered.

Cam moved beside Sandy, scooped up her fish, and brought it to the boat. Sandy sat her rod aside, took the pliers from Cam, and removed her hook before dumping the fish into the well.

"That's a good start. Let's do it again." Sandy grinned at Tab, then looked over at Cam. "You gonna join us?"

"In a bit. I want to make sure you two are all set."

Cam returned to her seat and watched them bait hooks and cast into the water. Her eyes surveyed the banks and she saw evidence of slide marks where some decent-sized gators had entered the water recently. She made a mental note to tell her dad the location for next year's gator season. Their bait had barely settled into the water when both Tab and Sandy had new fish hooked. She waited until Tab's fish was close, then scooped it up and handed her the pliers. She was tentative at first but finally managed to free the hook and drop the fish in the well.

"You've got it, now rinse, and repeat." She grinned and turned to net Sandy's fish. "You two are pulling them in so quick, I think I'll just be your net operator."

"Okay, Cam," Sandy said as Cam lifted an even larger fish out of the water.

"Oh, he's a big boy." Cam gave her baby sister a high five. "I'm going to get a workout just hauling the fish in for you two."

Sandy grinned up at Cam, and it was hard to tell which of the three of them was having the most fun. Tab let out an excited squeal every time she hooked a fish causing Cam and Sandy to laugh.

"Normally I'd say you're scaring the fish off with all that squealing, but it's apparent those darn fish are attracted to you and come to find out what on earth is going on," Cam teased.

"This is so much fun," Tab said.

Sandy grinned back at her. "Told ya so."

Tab's shoulders were turning pink, so Cam pulled a work shirt off the back of her seat and walked over to her. "Please slip this on. I really don't want you to be burned to a crisp on your first day."

Tab nodded and handed Cam her rod as she slipped into the shirt. "Thanks."

"You're welcome." Cam grabbed the net as Sandy brought in another fish. "At this rate, we're going to be done early today."

†

Two hours later, they had filled up the well.

"Let's go see what today's catch brings in," Cam said as she pulled up the anchor. She guided the boat into the docks at LB's, and Bren came down from the office to chat with Tab as Sandy and Cam unloaded the catch.

"It's good to see you again. Cam's been so excited to have you visit for the summer."

"Thanks, it's good to see you too. How's married life?" Tab asked.

"Going well so far. We've started building a house. If we get it done before y'all leave for school, you'll have to come to the housewarming."

"That sounds great. I'm already having a great time."

"From the look of it, y'all did well again today."

"Sandy's a good teacher, and I had a blast fishing with her."

"She'll keep ya busy fishing for a while. That kid loves to fish with Cam, but who can blame her? Cam's a great sister and friend."

"That she is. I'm so glad we met. Maybe you and Rudy can join us out on the Island sometime this summer."

"Oh, he'd love that." Bren chuckled.

Sandy rushed up to them, waving a receipt. "We did it, Tab. One-hundred-and-two pounds."

"That's awesome!" She gave Sandy a high five. "You're a great teacher, and I love fishing."

"I knew you would. You get half of today's catch too."

"Nope, they're all yours. I just came along to learn how to fish. Whatever we catch is all yours."

Sandy wrinkled up her nose in her adorable way. "But you caught at least half of them."

"Only because you're a great teacher. Anything I catch with you is just pure fun for me."

"Well, all right." Sandy rushed back to the boat.

She turned back to Bren, who was smiling. "That kid is pure fun. I hope to have a few just like her."

"She is a great kid," Tab agreed.

Cam waved to Bren. "You ready to roll, Tab? We still need to take your stuff out to the camp."

"I guess that's my cue to get moving. Good to see you again. I'm sure we'll see you tomorrow with more fish."

Bren chuckled. "I'll be looking forward to writing y'all a big check Friday. Have fun and I'll see you tomorrow."

"See ya." Tab walked quickly to the boat.

Cam offered her a hand to step down into it. "Let's head home, drop Sandy off, and take your bags out to the Island."

"Aww, I can't go?" Sandy groaned.

"Well, let's see what Mama's got planned for dinner, and we'll take it from there."

"Deal." Sandy grinned.

†

When they arrived back at home, Cam said, "Let's go wash up and see what the others are doing."

Sandy jumped onto the dock and secured the boat, and Tab removed the shirt and handed it back to Cam. "Better keep this for tomorrow."

Cam inspected her shoulders. "They are a little pink, but hopefully not too bad. I've got some aloe we can use on them after you shower tonight."

They walked up to the house just as Ronny and Wanda returned. They had delivered the corn picked earlier in the day and were carrying some grocery bags. He looked at them. "Are y'all up for a boil for supper?"

"Oh, heck yeah," Cam answered. "Do I need to go get some bugs?"

"Nope, me and Wanda brought home a couple extra buckets today, and your mama held back some fresh corn. Wanda and I picked up some sausage and potatoes while we were in town."

Cam smiled at him. "It sounds like we just need some cooking and eating, then."

"You've still got to get Tab settled in at camp, so Wanda and I'll start the boil in a bit. Will y'all be ready by seven?"

Cam looked at her watch. "That gives us plenty of time. Did you pick up beer?"

"I got a case in the back in a tub of ice if you gals wouldn't mind carrying it to the back for me."

"Not a problem, Dad." Cam and Tab walked to the truck and pulled open the tailgate. "You take that side, so you can use your good hand. How's it feeling, by the way?"

"It's good, still a bit stiff from being in the cast, but it's great to have it off."

"Let's get this set up and grab your bags. Do you mind Sandy riding over with us?"

"No, not at all. She's made this day very special for me."

"That feeling is quite mutual, I do believe. I know I'm stoked to have you here."

Sandy rushed out to meet them. "Mama said it was okay for me to ride out to the camp with ya, if it's good with you."

"Let us go wash our hands, then we'll grab Tab's bags. We gotta be back in time for a boil tonight."

"I know. I can hardly wait. I'm hungry."

"Let's get a move on, then."

†

They returned from the boil much later than Cam had intended, but Tab was having so much fun with her family that pulling her away was difficult. The boil had turned out great, and after a few Abitas, Cam was feeling very relaxed, but they still needed to shower and get in bed. Tomorrow would be another long day of cutting cane, then fishing. She had also agreed to help her dad cook tomorrow night, so she had to have a conversation with Tab about her family's moonshine activities. If they were lucky, they'd finish in time tomorrow for a short nap, since they would be up cooking until midnight or later.

After a quick shower, Cam spread some chilled aloe gel across Tab's shoulders, then went to the kitchen to grab two more cold beers and brought them into the bedroom.

Tab's eyes were beginning to droop, but Cam needed to talk to her tonight.

"I know you're probably whipped after a day out on the water, but there's something we need to discuss tonight."

Tab sat up in bed and took the beer Cam offered. "Okay, Cam. What's up?"

"The St. Angelo family has several family businesses, as you have already witnessed firsthand, but there is one you don't know about yet. For over a hundred years, our family has cooked some of the best 'shine in the area."

"'Shine, as in moonshine?"

"Yes, moonshine. The large shed out back, houses our family still, and several times a month, Dad and I will get together and cook batches of 'shine he sells primarily to two special customers. Tomorrow night we're supposed to be preparing a batch, and I wanted to talk to you in case you preferred not being here, because even though it's common in the swamp, it's still illegal."

Tab took a long drink from her beer. "I don't have any problem with that. In fact, I'd like to see how 'shine is cooked. If you've been cooking that long, I'd say the chances of you getting caught are slim."

"While we are cooking, yes. Our more dangerous time is during delivery, but Dad always handles that."

"Thanks for being honest with me. I've never tasted 'shine and I've certainly never seen it cooked. It'll be another new experience for me."

"You do understand it has to remain a secret."

"My lips are sealed, I promise."

"Good, because it is a large part of our family's income and I wouldn't want to jeopardize that or risk anyone going to jail."

"I would never dream of it. Your family is far too precious to me."

"Thank you. How are you feeling?"

"Exhausted, but at peace. I love being here with you and your family."

"You know I watched you and Sandy today fishing, and I don't know which of the three of us was happier."

"We were all right where we wanted to be. So, what's on tap for tomorrow?"

"After breakfast, we'll cut cane, then fish, and hopefully we can catch a quick nap before Dad comes over to cook. I hope you know we do not expect you to do any of the work. Especially cutting cane. It's hot, messy work."

"Ha! This city girl is going to do her best to hang with the country folk. Besides, I don't want to miss a minute with you."

"After tomorrow, the rest of the week will be a little easier, and we'll have some time to relax, I promise."

"Let's get some sleep, then, so we'll be ready to go."

Cam took their empty bottles into the kitchen and dropped them in the trash. Tab was already stretched out under the covers when she returned. She turned off the lamp and climbed into bed, and a sleepy Tab said, "Spoon me, please."

"With pleasure," she answered and molded her body around Tab. "Love you," she whispered.

"Love you too, Cam. Good night."

CHAPTER THREE

For the next few weeks, Tab experienced life with the St. Angelos and learned everything there was to know about cooking mash, fishing, and farming in bayou country. Logan and Wanda spent a long weekend with them at the camp and were excited to hear they would be attending the softball camp in July. The four sat down and talked about the feelings that were growing between Wanda and Logan. Cam tried to explain how difficult a lesbian relationship was at any age, but they seemed determined that their feelings were genuine, and Tab suspected Wanda and Logan did a bit of experimenting on their own that weekend. Life was good, and for the first time ever, she was enjoying summer.

Cam woke her with sweet loving the day before they were due to drive back to Baton Rouge to prepare for the first softball camp. When they stretched out on their backs afterward trying to catch their breath, Cam said, "Dress light today in something you don't mind getting dirty."

"That sounds interesting. What do you have planned?"

"It's time to feed the hogs."

"What hogs? I've never seen hogs here."

Cam chuckled. "You probably won't see any, either. They are crafty little creatures, but part of our income is generated by booking hunts for wild boar and deer on the Island. To keep them well fed and reproducing, we feed them throughout the summer. So today, we're going four-wheeling deep into the Island to fill the feeders."

"What do we feed them?"

"A mixture of dried corn and sweet feed. But where we're going, you're likely to get a bit muddy."

"That sounds like fun."

"Will you make us some sandwiches and pack a small cooler while I go across the water to pick up the feed from Dad?"

"Do I need to plan for more than two?"

"That would be a good possibility. I'll be lucky if I can get back here with just Wanda and Squirt."

"Four, then?"

"Yes, four." Cam grinned. "Do you mind sharing the adventure with those two? I can tell them no."

"Don't even consider that. They have you only for such a short while, and I couldn't dream of depriving them of Cam time."

"Thanks, honey." Cam kissed her sweetly before climbing out of bed. "Do you want to shower with me?"

"Want to, yes, but it would probably take us a lot longer." Tab smiled.

"Good point. I'll hurry so I can get across the water and get loaded."

"I'll go ahead and pack some drinks in the cooler and make the sandwiches after I shower."

†

Cam could see movement at the homeplace as she crossed the water. When she reached the docks, Wanda, Sandy, and her dad waited for her.

"Good morning," she said as she got out of the boat and approached. "Y'all are up bright and early."

Ronny ruffled Sandy's hair. "These two knuckleheads were up at dawn when they heard you were feeding hogs today. I don't suppose you and Tab would mind a little company?"

"Tab's already making sandwiches for four."

"Work them hard, then," Ronny teased as Sandy tied off her boat.

"You got any chores for us this afternoon?" Cam asked.

"Nope, we're caught up for a minute."

"Better grab another rod and some bait, then," she told Sandy and Wanda. "We might as well do some fishing later on. Oh, and run inside for a fresh change of clothes. I plan on getting dirty." She grinned.

"Now we're talking." Sandy ran for the bait while Wanda grabbed another rod and reel, then they both disappeared into the house and returned with a change of clothes each.

Ronny handed five, fifty-pound bags of feed over to Cam. "I'd ask if ya needed help, but you're gonna have your hands full."

"Thanks, Dad. I'll have them home before dark. Are we cooking tonight?"

"Naw, T said she'd help me next week while y'all are gone back to Baton Rouge."

"Okay, then. I reckon we'll see you later."

"Your mama's cooking up spaghetti, so don't be too late."

"Yes, sir."

Ronny tossed Wanda the line, and Cam pulled away from the dock.

†

As Tab made sandwiches for their trip, she thought about how this summer was one of the best she'd ever had. She and Cam would only be gone for two weeks for the first camp, but she would miss the days spent with Cam and her newfound family as they worked together. She was lost in fond memories when she heard the roar of the boat's motor as it pulled into the canal. Moments later she heard laughter as Cam and her sisters approached the cabin.

Wanda was the first through the door, and Sandy followed closely. Cam stuck her head in to grab a set of keys from a hook on the wall. "These two are going to help you finish up while I grab the Gator and load the feed and some buckets. Drop your clothes in the spare bedroom."

"Okay, I'm almost done here. Wanda, will you pull out a bag of chips, and Sandy, will you help Wanda carry the cooler out to the Gator? I'll bring the chips and sandwiches."

"You got it, boss," Sandy teased.

Tab shot her a grin as she wrapped the last of the sandwiches, then tucked them in a small satchel and followed them out the door.

"I'll be right back," Cam said after pulling the loaded Gator in front of the cabin. She rushed inside and returned with her pistol on her belt. "I hope we won't need it, but you never know," she said to herself then she climbed in beside Tab. Cam turned to the backseat and asked, "All set?"

"Ready to go," Wanda answered.

"Hold on tight, then. It might get bumpy." She chuckled and started the Gator, then looked over at Tab. "Is this another first for you?"

"Riding in a Gator and feeding hogs are both new to me, so treat me gently."

"Hey, Cam, maybe we should take her snipe hunting while she's here this summer," Wanda chimed in and Sandy giggled.

"Snipe hunting?"

"Hmm, that's not a bad idea. Maybe after we get back from camp," Cam answered.

"What's a snipe?"

"A crafty little bird that only comes out at night, but my goodness they are some tasty eating. Speaking of which, Mama's making spaghetti tonight."

"Yummy, I love Mama's spaghetti," Sandy said.

"Hang on," Cam cried out and ran the Gator through a muddy puddle. Water splashed up the sides of the four-wheeler, and Tab got her first taste of bayou mud.

"Oops, I reckon I shoulda warned ya to watch the splash." Cam chuckled as Tab wiped the mud from her arm.

Tab shot her a grin. "I reckon you shoulda."

†

For the next half hour, Cam expertly guided the Gator down worn trails until they reached the first of the feeders. Tab assumed they would fill the large aluminum bin that was open at the bottom with feed. Cam pulled up close to it, and her sisters jumped out of the backseat to hold two five-gallon buckets as Cam filled them with feed. "Why the mixture?" Tab asked as the girls mixed the corn and sweet feed into the buckets.

"The corn to fatten them up, and the sweet feed is full of molasses, which hogs can't resist. By the time hunting season rolls around, they'll be nice and filled out. Toss a little bit on the ground for piglets and to feed the snipe," Cam told Sandy with a wink.

"We have to come out here to hunt snipe?" Tab asked innocently.

"Naw, they will have migrated closer to the cabin by the time we get back. We'll have feeders set up just for them." She turned to wink at Wanda.

Wanda and Sandy could barely contain their laughter as they mixed the feed and handed their buckets to Cam to pour into the feeder. Cam emptied each one and turned back to them. "That's one down; three more to go."

On their way to the next feeder, Cam slowed as a doe and twins crossed the path ahead of them. "Aren't they pretty?"

"Yes, but I can't believe someone could shoot them," Tab said.

"Only the big males, sweetheart," Cam promised. "If we don't take some of the bucks, then they will overpopulate and the weaker ones will go hungry and die."

"I know, but still." Tab frowned. "Have you killed many?"

"One or two," Cam admitted. "We always eat what we kill, and if we have more than we need, the extra meat goes to help other families."

"At least it doesn't go to waste."

"No, we would never let that happen." Cam refrained from telling her that the wealthy men, who came out to hunt, only wanted the big racks for trophies and weren't interested at all for the meat. She was telling the truth, though, when she said it never went to waste.

They moved on and when they had the final feeder filled, they ate lunch at a quiet meadow, then started for home.

"You might want to hold on tight through this next spot," Cam warned as she drove into a shallow bog. The Gator slid from side to side, slinging mud in every direction. Wanda and Sandy hollered in the backseat as the Gator dropped into a hole and muddy water flew over the hood, soaking the passengers. "Damn, that was deeper than I thought."

Tab grinned back at her, still wiping her face. "Yeah, I bet it was."

†

"Sandy, take the buckets back to the boat and then you and Wanda use the guest room shower to get cleaned up," Cam instructed after they'd pulled back into the yard. "Wanda, throw these feedbags in the fire pit. You can go ahead and shower too," she told Tab.

"What are you going to do?"

"I'm going to rinse off the Gator and put it back in the shed. Someone got her all dirty today." She chuckled. "It sure was fun."

"Yes, it was. Thanks for another new experience."

"My pleasure, ma'am. Hopefully there will be many more to come. Save me some hot water." She grinned as she picked up the hose and turned on the water. Sandy was walking back toward them, and Cam couldn't resist shooting the cold water at her baby sister. "Gotcha, Squirt," she said as Sandy squealed.

"Yeah, you did, Cam." Sandy hid behind Tab for protection.

"Do you really think that's going to save you?"

"Don't you dare, Cam," Tab warned.

Cam thought about the implications soaking Tab and Sandy could bring, and wisely thought better of her threat. "You better get inside before I change my mind, then," she said with a wink at Tab.

"That's the best decision you've made all day," Tab said.

"Go on now, before I change my mind."

Sandy and Tab took off running for the cabin, laughing all the way inside. She turned the hose to the Gator. "Damn, but we had fun." She rinsed it, still smiling at the look on Tab's face when the muddy water splashed into the four-wheeler. When it was sufficiently clean, Cam drove it back to the shed and hung the keys back inside the cabin door when she entered. Sandy was already showered and sitting at the table working on the jigsaw puzzle.

"I thought you'd have it done by now," she said when she looked up at Cam.

"I've been messing with it some, but thought I'd work on it more with you."

Sandy smiled. "I bet you've just been too busy with Tab."

"Well, that, too, but I really enjoy puzzling with you." Cam heard the water in her shower turn off. "I reckon I better get a move on so we can get to fishing."

"Yep, daylight's a-wasting," Sandy teased.

"Such a slave driver," Cam groaned and went into her bedroom as Sandy laughed. She found Tab drying off in the bathroom and held her arms out for a hug.

"Don't even think about it, Cam St. Angelo," Tab warned. "Get out of those dirty clothes and in the shower. I'll drop our clothes in the washer before we leave."

Cam stripped and snuck a quick kiss from Tab before she climbed into the shower. "Man, I was dirty," she said as the water rinsed the mud from her body.

"I can't imagine how that happened," Tab said. "I'm going to get dressed."

"Okay, sweetie."

Tab stood at the sink brushing her teeth, wearing shorts and a sports bra. She had gained a dark tan over the last few weeks and a sprinkling of freckles across her shoulders. The hard work had firmed up her arms and shoulders, and the movement of her muscles as she brushed her teeth mesmerized Cam. Tab bent over to rinse her mouth and straightened to find Cam watching her.

"Like what you see?"

"Nope, I love what I see. I think working out here has buffed you up even more than before. I may have to beat the women away from you when we get back to school."

"You are so funny, but I think you're right," she said as she flexed her arms. "I've got guns."

Cam stepped out of the shower chuckling. "Yes, you do."

✝

When they walked out to the boat, Cam handed Wanda the keys.

"What's this about?"

"Someone's got to drive Sandy around to fish while we're gone to camp, so it might as well be you. You need to practice and today's as good as any to start. T or Karen can drive her while you're gone to camp, but you need to learn."

"I hadn't thought about that," Sandy said.

"The fishing still needs to happen and Dad doesn't have time to drive you around, so it's going to be up to you two to get it done. Think y'all can handle that?"

"Heck yeah," Wanda said.

"I'll even split my earnings with you if you help me fish," Sandy offered.

Cam smiled at her sisters. "That sounds like a good deal. You've got to be very careful with Dad's boat. No racing or reckless driving. That means no showing off if Logan joins you for a day or two."

"I got this, Cam."

"Show me," she said and stepped into the boat.

CHAPTER FOUR

The summer passed too quickly for Cam. The softball camps went smoothly and Coach was impressed with Wanda and Logan. Cam couldn't wipe the smile off her face as she watched the two young girls interacting, and she felt sure their relationship had grown from mere friendship to something more.

"I guess I was just a late bloomer," she told Tab as they snuggled on the last night of camp.

Tab chuckled. "You may have started late, but you certainly have blossomed. Wanda and Logan are blessed to have an older role model to look up to and ask questions of. That may have been what was missing for you."

"Maybe so, or maybe I was just waiting for you."

"You say some of the sweetest things sometimes." Tab snuggled into her.

†

The next morning, they loaded up the girls and headed home. Cam and Tab would have two more weeks together before Tab went back to Monroe to spend the last week of their break with her parents.

As she pulled into the drive, Tab looked over at Cam. "I sure am going to miss this place."

"You know you're welcome anytime. I hope you've had a great summer."

"The best summer of my life. I've learned so much from you and your family, and experienced things I never would have in Monroe."

"It has been a great summer. I wish it would never end, but we have lots to do when we get back to school."

Tab didn't want to think of school. When they returned, she would be entering her junior year, and after graduating, she would be off to Duke to start law school. Her application for admission to their law program had already been approved by the university. Tab was uncertain of being able to maintain a long-distance romance with Cam. She pushed those thoughts to the back of her mind, intent on enjoying the time they had together.

"Can Logan spend the weekend with us?"

Cam looked at Logan. "You want to call home and see if it's okay?"

"Sure, I'd love that."

Tab smiled at Cam. "We have ingredients for s'mores, and I think it's time we had a campfire."

"That sounds like the perfect way to end a great week," she replied. "You want to join us too, Squirt?"

"That's a silly question," Sandy answered. "Of course, I do. I can't wait to break in my new rod and reel, either."

Cam smiled at how pleased Sandy was with the birthday gift from her and Tab. "I think we can all fit on the boat if you want to fish after lunch."

"I bet there are fish out there just waiting for you to hook them," Tab added.

As the car rolled to a stop, Cam turned toward the backseat. "Let's get unloaded. Logan, you can call home while we see what Mama's got for lunch, then we'll go over to the Island."

†

They finished off the day of fishing with a cookout and campfire. Cam grilled burgers, while Tab and Wanda cooked fries. After supper Cam lit the campfire and they cooked s'mores and enjoyed the gooey treats. Sandy, worn out from all the excitement, fell asleep in Cam's lap.

"I think I'll take her inside and get her settled on the couch," she whispered to Tab. "We shouldn't be far behind her. We can give them some time alone together." She nodded toward Wanda and Logan.

Tab smiled at the sight of the two sitting close together. "Okay, I'll wait for you to come back, then we'll head inside too."

Cam carried Sandy into the cabin, placed her on the couch, and covered her with a light blanket. She stirred briefly to look up at Cam.

"Love you, Cam," she whispered.

"Love you too, Squirt. Sweet dreams."

When she walked back outside, Wanda and Logan were holding hands. "Tab and I are going to bed. Will you make sure the fire is out before you come in?" she asked Wanda.

"Sure will."

"Don't stay out too late. Dad wants us to deliver mud bugs to LB's tomorrow."

"We won't," she promised.

Cam reached for Tab's hand. "Ready?"

"Good night, girls," Tab said. "Have fun."

"You too." Logan grinned.

†

Tab's bags were packed and she was ready to begin her ride back to Monroe.

"I miss you already," she told Cam.

"Hopefully the week will pass quickly and I'll see you in Baton Rouge this weekend. I plan to go back early Saturday morning."

"I'll be there as fast as I can."

"Be safe and call me later."

"You can bet on that," Tab promised. "Thanks again for a wonderful summer."

"I enjoyed every minute of it." Cam pulled her close and kissed her softly. "I love you."

"Love you too. See you soon."

Tab had tears in her eyes as she climbed behind the wheel. The screen door slammed and Cam turned to see Sandy rushing toward them. She stopped beside Cam and looked at Tab.

"Thanks for staying with us this summer. I had a lot of fun with you."

"I did too, Squirt. Take care of Cam for me."

"I will, Tab. Be safe. See you soon, I hope."

"Definitely for a ball game this fall. We're gonna have a great team this year."

"Awesome." Sandy took Cam's hand.

"Be safe," Cam repeated.

Tab nodded and drove down the driveway, waving as she reached the highway. Cam and Sandy waved, and Cam looked down at Sandy and saw that her eyes filled with tears.

"Let's go see what Dad has planned for us today," Cam said and punched her lightly in the shoulder.

†

Cam cooked 'shine with her dad every night that week to get him ahead of schedule. Sandy had amassed a nice bit of savings from her summer fishing job and wanted Cam to take her shopping for some new school clothes.

They arrived at a local department store and Cam grabbed a cart. "Where do we start?"

"I need some new uniforms for school. I've grown out of last year's."

"You are getting big," Cam agreed.

They passed the sporting-goods section on the way and Sandy saw a T-shirt that said, "Fish Fear Me" and looked up at Cam. "Can I buy one of these for Tab?"

"She'd love that."

"Will you select one her size?"

Cam chuckled at the image of a fish cowering in fear and picked out a shirt and handed it to Sandy, who placed it in the cart with great pride. "She's going to love it, I know."

"Yes, she will."

After they found Sandy's school uniforms, Cam looked at her. "What else?"

"I need some new jeans and shorts. A few new shirts wouldn't hurt, either."

"How about shoes?"

"Yes, shoes too."

When they exited the store, Sandy was pleased and proud that she still had money left. "Can I buy us a hamburger for lunch?"

"Sure, that sounds good."

Cam pulled into a fast-food chain restaurant and they went inside. "You order and I'll get us a seat."

Sandy was clearly pleased that Cam thought she was mature enough to order on her own. She marched up to the counter and placed their orders while Cam got napkins and condiments.

A few minutes later Sandy carried a tray of food loaded with burgers and fries to the table.

"Were you hungry?" Cam teased.

"I thought we could eat two each." She grinned. "Shopping is hard work."

"That it is, Squirt," Cam said as she stood and picked up their drink cups. "What do you want to drink?"

"A Coke for me, please."

They ate and returned to the Jeep, and Sandy climbed in and fastened her seatbelt. "What time are you planning to leave tomorrow?"

"Early. Right after breakfast. Why?"

"I didn't want to miss saying goodbye."

"Well, that's not going to happen. I need you and Wanda to spend the night with me tonight so you can help me bring my bags to the Jeep."

"That sounds good to me."

†

Cam spent the evening around the campfire with Sandy and Wanda, making s'mores and talking about the fun they'd shared over the summer. When Sandy's eyes grew heavy, she said, "I think it's time we wrap this up and head into bed. Wanda, if you'll dispose of the trash, I'll put the fire out."

"Deal," Wanda answered.

Cam walked over to Sandy and leaned down to kiss her forehead. "Get some sleep and I'll see you in the morning."

"Good night Cam," she said, stifling a yawn. "Love you."

"I love you too. Good night." Sandy walked into the cabin.

Wanda finished picking up and turned to Cam, who was dowsing the fire. "Is there anything else I can help with?"

"Nope, I've got it from here." Cam hugged her close. "We had a great summer, didn't we?"

"Yes, we did. I hope we have many more like that. It was fun having Tab and Logan share parts of it with us."

Cam smiled. "Yes, it was. Get some rest and I'll see you in the morning."

"Good night, Cam. Love you."

"Love you too."

Cam watched her enter the cabin and sat down in her chair to watch the final embers fade. The sounds of the bayou returned unbroken by their laughter and she wondered if they would have another summer like this one.

"Almost perfect," she said. Cam enjoyed the nighttime symphony for several minutes, then stood to poke at the fire to ensure the coals were cooling down, before walking to her room. Instinctively she picked up her phone and found she had missed a call from Tab. She smiled and hit the button to return the call.

"I hope I didn't wake you," she said when Tab answered. "I miss you too, but I'll see you soon." She chuckled. "I know, it's not soon enough for me, either." She listened to Tab for several minutes. "Yes, Sandy, Wanda, and I made s'mores and small talk around the fire tonight. I'm not the only one who misses you." She chuckled at Tab's comment. "Yes, I know those two are following in my footsteps. Wanda is totally smitten with Logan, and Sandy has goo-goo eyes for you."

She frowned as Tab told her about the icy homecoming she received from her mother, but that she had the best summer of her life. "Yes, I know. We were talking about how great a summer it was tonight. There will be more, I promise. … Okay, love, I'll see you soon. … Love you too."

†

Cam woke early the next morning, showered, dressed, and was packing the last of her bags when a groggy Wanda walked into her room. "Good morning."

"Good morning. Do you really have to go back today?"

The plea in Wanda's voice made Cam's heart ache. "Yeah, I do. We all need to get ready to start a new school year."

Wanda ran a hand through her hair. "Don't remind me. Dang, this summer sure went by fast."

"Yes, it did, but there's one good thing about starting back to school."

Wanda looked up at her with interest.

"You get to see Logan every day."

Her puzzled look changed into a grin. "There is that. We won't have classes together but have lunch the same period. We've both decided to play volleyball and basketball this year, so we'll spend time together during practice."

"That's a good plan. Don't forget about keeping your grades up. I think Coach was very impressed with your skills this summer and will save a spot on the team for you if you still want to play in college."

"Heck yeah. Too bad you'll have graduated already. It would have been cool to play on the same team as you."

"Yes, it would. I'll do my best to keep the St. Angelo name in good status," she teased.

"At the top of all the record books, I hope."

"I'm going to give it my best shot. Go get your lazybones sister up so we can get across the water in time for breakfast."

"I'm up," Sandy said as she entered the room.

"Get your shoes on and y'all can help me carry these bags out to the boat."

Cam smiled as they shuffled out of the room. Sadness came over her at having to leave her family behind, but she was eager to return to school to be with Tab. She picked up two bags and walked toward the door when her sisters returned. "Grab some bags and let's get this show moving."

Cam walked out to a beautiful bayou morning, the cool ground fog still clinging to the veils of Spanish moss hanging from the trees. It had receded from the water when the sun rose and would conceal the depths of the Island until the sun burned it away within the hour.

"Home," she whispered, then turned back when the door to the cabin creaked open and Sandy and Wanda emerged, loaded down with bags.

"We got all but one," Wanda said as she passed them on her way to the boat.

"I'll grab it and lock up."

Cam entered the cabin and glanced at the jigsaw puzzle on the table. Sandy had gotten up during the night to finish it and left the last piece for her. She picked it up and smiled as she slipped it into place, completing the scene of a beautiful bayou, with cypress trees standing guard, their limbs highlighted by a beautiful sunrise.

"Home," she repeated and went to the room for her last bag. She carried it out and stopped to lock the door, then handed the bag down to Wanda. Sandy was standing on the dock, mooring line in hand, and when Cam stepped onboard, Sandy pushed off and followed her onto the boat.

"Are you two going to do some more fishing until school starts?"

Sandy gave her a lopsided grin. "As long as we can, if Dad doesn't need us for chores."

"Things will calm down a bit now the summer harvests are slowing down, so I bet you can get more fishing done."

"I hope so," Sandy said.

"Take us home," Cam told Wanda as she handed her the keys to the boat.

"You got it." Wanda expertly drove the boat across the bayou, where she docked at the homestead.

"Great job," Cam said as Wanda shut down the boat. "Tie us off, Squirt, and let's get the Jeep loaded and see what Mama's got cooking."

†

After a tearful goodbye, Cam climbed into her Jeep to drive to Baton Rouge. It broke her heart every time Sandy cried when she left, and she worried that leaving her family behind would never grow easier. She stopped at the end of the drive to wave one last time to Sandy, who was still furiously waving with one hand while wiping her tears with the other.

The morning was beautiful as she turned on her blinker and turned right onto the highway. A blue heron flew across the road in front of her, a small fish trapped in its beak. *That's one less Sandy will be catching today.* She shifted gears as she drove through the bayou. No matter how many times she traveled this route, Cam marveled at the scenery: the cypress knees poking out of the water, and the bountiful wildlife continuing on their daily routines to survive life on the bayou. No matter where life took her, this would always be home.

†

The next week would be full as she registered for classes, welcomed the new players to campus, and settled back into college life. The best part was knowing that whenever she returned to their apartment, Tab would be there, and they would enjoy the last week before classes would resume. Fall conditioning would begin in a few weeks, and she and Tab hung the poster and T-shirt they'd bought at the College World Series in the field house, to remind the team that their goal for the year was to make it to Oklahoma City.

Life was good. The football season had begun, and Sandy and Wanda joined them for a game. Wanda seemed a bit off, though, not as excited as she usually was, and after they returned for pizza with Ruth and Liz, she asked Cam if they could talk. They went back to her apartment and sat down together on the couch.

"What's up? You haven't been yourself all day."

The dam holding back Wanda's tears burst and she leaned into Cam. Cam held her close, whispering soothing words until Wanda stopped crying. "What's going on?"

Wanda sat up and wiped her eyes. "Logan's mom is taking her away."

"What?"

"She's got a job offer in Indiana, so Logan will be leaving at Christmas break to move with her."

"Oh, Wanda, I'm so sorry to hear that." Cam wrapped her arms around her. "There's no way she can at least finish out the school year and then move?"

"No, we already asked. Her Mom is adamant that she leaves at Christmas."

"That really stinks. I wish I knew something to help ease the pain, but that's all a part of the process of loving someone. The risk of being separated from the one you love."

"I know, Cam. Just when I thought life was really great, fate steps in to kick me in the teeth."

Cam really didn't know what else to say. "I understand how first loves are very special. I don't know what I'd do if something happened between Tab and me." For once, Cam really didn't have life experiences to fall back on in attempting to console her sister. "I could say there will be other loves and heartaches in your life, but that does so little to soothe the pain you're feeling right now."

"Logan didn't even know her mom was planning something like this."

"Sometimes adults don't feel it's necessary to share information that is likely to cause upset feelings until they are certain of the plan."

"It would have been nice to know so we could have spent more time together this summer. I'm not sure if it would have made it better or worse, though."

"Think of it this way. If her mom had known back then, Logan may not have even started back to school with you this year. You had some awfully good times together this summer. Those will be cherished memories for you."

"Yeah, I know."

"Logan will graduate next year, so maybe she'll come back down to go to LSU."

"You are an optimist, Cam. I have a feeling when we say goodbye, it will be forever."

"That's always a possibility, but you can still remain long-distance friends."

"I just wish we were all grown-up and could make our own decisions," Wanda said between sniffles.

"Trust me when I say being grown-up isn't what it's made out to be. In some ways, it would be so much easier to be back at home without a worry in the world."

"But then you wouldn't have met Tab." Wanda frowned.

"There is that." Cam smiled. "You want us to hang out here for a bit?"

"Naw, let's go back to the others. I just needed to get that off my chest."

"I hope you know you can call and talk to me anytime."

Wanda hugged her again. "Yeah, I do, and I'm so glad to have you as a big sister."

"Well I couldn't be prouder to call you my little sis. Come on, let's go see if there's a slice or two of pizza left."

†

The redness in Wanda's eyes gave away the fact she'd been crying, but no one mentioned it when they returned. Tab smiled sweetly at Cam, and she really did wonder how she would react to losing Tab. The somber thought reminded her that Tab indeed would be moving away to attend law school after she graduated. They had discussed it only briefly, and Cam was worried a long-distance relationship wouldn't work well for them. Still, they had this year and next to make the most of life and they were determined to give it their all.

CHAPTER FIVE

Three months later, Cam had finished her finals for the day and walked back to her apartment to drop off her backpack and change for the afternoon workout session. She wasn't aware her father was planning to visit, so seeing his truck parked next to her Jeep was a total shock. She rushed up the steps of the apartment complex and found him waiting for her in the lobby. When Ronny looked up at her arrival, his eyes were ringed with dark circles and filled with sadness. Her heart plummeted to her belly, forming a knot of dread.

He stood and she rushed to hug him. "I wasn't expecting you, but I'm always glad to see you."

Ronny forced a smile. "I know, honey. I should have called to let you know I was coming. We need to talk."

"Is everything all right?"

"Can we go up to your apartment?"

"Yes, sure. I'm sorry, come on up."

They climbed the stairs to the apartment she shared with Tab, and she was glad her lover had already left for practice.

Cam closed the door behind them and had him sit at the small table she and Tab shared. "Can I get you something to drink?"

"Not right now, honey. Come sit with me."

Cam's knees felt weak and she welcomed the solid chair beneath her. "What's wrong, Dad? You look terrible."

Ronny took a deep breath, and tears filled his eyes. "There's no easy way to tell you this, but your mama is sick. She's dying, Cam, and there's not a damned thing I can do about it."

Cam felt her face blanch. "What? What are you saying?"

"She's been feeling poorly now for a few weeks. I brought her to Baton Rouge day before yesterday to see a specialist." He choked up, trying and failing to speak for several seconds. "She's got an aggressive form of pancreatic cancer."

Cam wasn't well versed in medical conditions, but her dad's expression told her how serious this was. "Isn't there anything we can do?" she murmured, feeling cold and weak all over.

"It's too late. The cancer has already spread. The doctor has no way of telling, but he's given her one to two months tops." He broke down crying, and Cam moved to kneel next to him and hugged him close.

"I'm so sorry, Dad." She had no other words to speak. "I didn't even realize she was sick when I was home for Thanksgiving."

"She's been hiding her illness from you kids. Didn't want y'all to worry, you know how your mama is."

"Yes, sir, I do."

He wiped the tears from his eyes as Cam rested back on her heels. "I hate to ask this of you, but I've run out of options. I need you to come home, Cam. I've dreaded asking you to leave school ever since we found out, but I simply can't handle running the house and the businesses by myself. I need your help with your mama and your sisters."

Stunned, Cam remained silent as his pleas sunk in. "Of course, I'll come home. I've got one other final tomorrow. I'll make arrangements and be home Saturday morning. Is that soon enough?"

"Yes, that will be fine. You don't know how much that means to me. I hate to ask you to place your studies on hold, but we need you."

"College will just have to wait. Do the girls know?"

"Only T. I wanted to wait until you came home to tell the others. She was devastated, so I imagine the others will be too."

"Especially Squirt. She's going to take it hard."

"That's more the reason I have to ask this of you. She worships the ground you walk on and having you there will hopefully ease her pain."

"Yes, I agree. She's so young to experience this kind of trauma."

"I hope you will be able to return to school next fall. I know this will probably cause you to lose your scholarship, but I have no other options."

"Don't worry Dad. Family always comes first. If it works out that I can return then I'll see if I can renew my scholarship, but right now my family is more important than playing ball."

His tears returned, and Cam began to cry. Her parents had been high school sweethearts, married for over twenty years. She could only imagine the heartache he was going through. Then the thought struck her that she would be saying goodbye to Tab. They had only been lovers for a little more than a year, but the thought of parting was further devastation. Sure, it was a short trip from Baton Rouge, but Cam wouldn't ask that of Tab. She only had one more year of college after this, and she needed to focus on school, not a relationship strained by absence.

When Ronny was able to dry his tears, he looked at Cam. "I really am sorry."

"I am too, Dad."

He nodded and pushed back from the table as Cam stood. "I'd better be getting back. See you Saturday."

Cam grabbed her keys. "I'll walk you out."

She hugged her dad when they reached the truck. "Be careful. I'll be home soon."

"I love you, Cam."

"Love you too."

Cam stepped back to allow him to climb into the truck and watched him drive away. Her heart ached for him and the devastation he must be feeling. She looked at her watch. She was twenty minutes late for practice, but there was no need to change into workout clothes. She needed to talk to Coach and Tab, to find out what she needed to do to withdraw from school.

†

When she walked into the workout room, Tab looked up and saw her. Judging by her frown as she rushed over to Cam, Tab could tell she had been crying. "What's wrong?"

"Dad came to visit. Mama's sick and I need to go home. I'll tell you everything in a bit, but I need to speak with Coach first, okay?"

"Sure." Tab pulled her into a tight hug. "I'm here no matter what."

Cam turned away quickly before the tears started falling and walked over to where her coach was working with another player. She looked up at Cam, startled by her appearance and her eyes widened. She could probably tell Cam had been crying and was upset.

"Can we talk in your office, Coach?"

"Sure, Cam. Let's go."

Cam closed the door behind them and sat across from her coach. "My dad was waiting for me today when I got done with a final. My mama is dying, and I need to go home to help him with her care and to take care of my sisters."

"Oh Cam, I am so sorry to hear that," she said and walked around to hug her. "What can I do?"

"Tell me what I need to do to withdraw from school."

"You don't need to worry about that. We'll make all the arrangements for you to take the time off. Don't worry about your scholarship. If you can come back, next fall or whenever, it will still be available."

That announcement was a spark of hope in a dismal day, but Cam feared she'd never return.

"Thanks, Coach. That means a lot to me."

"You're a great person as well as a great athlete. I hope you know you can call to talk anytime you want. I'll be here for you, whatever you need."

Cam choked back tears and nodded. "I've got one more final tomorrow, and I'll go home Saturday."

Coach hugged her again. "You're strong, Cam, probably one of the strongest players I've ever coached. Your family is lucky to have you for support."

"I appreciate that Coach. Hopefully I'll be talking to you soon."

"Anytime, day or night, remember that, please. You have my cell number, right?"

Cam nodded. "Yes, I do."

Coach walked her out of the office and nodded to Tab. "You're all done for the day."

"Thanks, Coach," Tab answered, and placed an arm around Cam's shoulders as they left the building.

†

Tab waited until they returned to the apartment and sat on her bed before asking Cam what had happened. With tears streaming down her cheeks, Cam laid out the details of her dad's visit. "I don't understand how this could happen to such a sweet woman," Tab said in shock.

"It's still hard to believe. Dad was crushed."

"I can only imagine. They've been in love for ages."

Cam sighed. "Which brings us to our relationship. I don't know if I'll ever make it back here. I love you with all my heart, but I want you to move on with your life."

Tab looked at her in surprise. "What? What about my opinion on this matter? Do I not have a voice here?"

"Of course you do, Tab, but you need to focus on school and playing ball, not running back and forth between campus and my home. We wouldn't be as free to be who we are in my home."

"I think you're selling your family short. They've seen us together and know we're in love."

Cam sighed. "I just don't see us together long-term. What happens when you graduate and move on to law school? What then? It's even farther away. Sandy's only nine years old and needs me."

"You don't think Teresa will be able to take over after she graduates this year?"

"T and Buster already have wedding plans for June. She needs to move on with her life too."

"So just because you're the oldest, you don't deserve a life?"

"I'll have a life, but my plans will just be put on hold for now."

Tab was trying to be supportive but couldn't hold back her anger. "So just like that your needs become inconsequential? You're expected to walk away from me like there's nothing between us?"

Cam broke down crying.

"Dammit, Cam, I didn't mean for it to sound that harsh. I'm sorry."

"That is the brutal truth of reality, though, Tab. I love you with all my heart, but I won't be able to give you what you need."

"Will you let me be the judge of that? Can we at least try to make this situation work?"

Cam sniffled. "Why would you want to?"

"Because, Cameron St. Angelo, I love you too with all my heart." She lifted Cam's chin and leaned in to kiss her.

†

Later that evening as Cam and Tab were packing, Liz and Ruth dropped in with pizza and beer. Coach had called the team together, to break the news to them after Cam had left the building.

"We're so sorry to hear about your mama," Liz said as she twisted off the cap to a beer and handed it to Cam.

"Thanks, Liz, and thanks for coming by with food, you guys."

"You are part of the best infield ever," Ruth, Liz's lover, former teammate, and now a graduate assistant, replied. "We're going to miss the hell out of you and hope you'll be able to return soon."

Cam took a sip of the beer and nibbled on a slice of pizza. Her appetite had disappeared.

Liz asked, "Is there anything we can do to help?"

"Thanks. Tab and I pretty much have things packed up. I'm heading home Saturday morning."

Ruth grinned. "One last beer bash tomorrow night before you go?"

Cam forced a smile. "Our usual spot on the river?"

"Where else? I'll even offer to be the designated driver to keep us out of trouble."

"Damn, this is serious if she's offering to be DD," Tab teased. "You up for it?"

"Sure, might as well make the best of my last night here, and there's no better friends than the three of y'all."

†

Later that evening when their friends left, Cam snuggled into bed with Tab.

"I'm going to miss this," she whispered.

"I'll come over every chance I get."

Cam remained silent until Tab rolled over on her side. "Are you up to making love tonight?"

"Yes, I'd like that."

Tab leaned down to kiss her as she slipped her hand beneath Cam's large T-shirt. She slowly and tenderly caressed Cam's stomach, her fingers brushing against Cam's breasts. "I think we need to lose these clothes."

Tab sat up to remove her shirt, then helped Cam slide hers over her head. She moved to lie carefully atop Cam, as if she'd suddenly become fragile. Cam chuckled, realizing Tab was trying to be gentle and pulled her down. "C'mere, you big brute, and love me like you mean it. I'm not a china doll."

Tab laughed until Cam's mouth covering hers choked out the laughter.

†

Sensing this might be one of the last times they would make love, Cam took special care to caress her lover's body, memorizing each fantastic inch of her for the lonely days and nights to come. Tab had vowed to do whatever she could to keep their love alive, but Cam knew the reality of the emotional roller coaster ahead for her, and doubted their relationship could weather the storm, or the distance between them. She was thankful the darkness hid the tears that flowed down her cheeks as they made love into the night.

†

Cam had prepared well for her last final, and when she turned in the exam, she felt like it was her last shot at college sliding through her hands. When she returned to the apartment, the pile of boxes waiting to be loaded into her

Jeep brought tears to her eyes. She felt selfish for crying for herself when her mama and family needed her.

Tab stepped into the room and took Cam in her arms and kissed her tenderly.

"I'm really going to miss our little love nest," Cam sniffled.

"Where will you stay at the house?"

"I may sleep out at the camp, at least until the time grows near, and then I'll sleep on the couch. I don't want to disrupt the family any more than necessary."

"I don't envy y'all telling the girls, especially Wanda and Sandy."

"I'm not looking forward to that, either," Cam said as tears flowed down her cheeks. "I'll be up early to make sure everyone gets off to school and then will care for Mama. I'll keep up the house with the girls' help and make sure everyone is fed well before retiring to the camp."

Tab brushed the hair from Cam's face. "Would it be okay if I come down for Christmas?"

"I'm not sure how festive it will be, but you're always welcome."

"I'll plan to come down early and leave Christmas Eve if that's okay? Mother will pitch a fit if I'm not home for Christmas."

"I'll treasure any time I have with you."

"Would you let me take you out for a nice dinner before we head out to the river?"

"I look like such a mess," Cam complained.

"No, you don't, honey. You look great in those jeans and oxfords. Just wash your face to freshen up and you'll be perfect."

"Give me a few minutes, then."

"I'll call and make a reservation. I love you, Cam."
"Love you too."

†

They shared a quiet evening at the river with Liz and Ruth, but her mama's illness weighed heavily on Cam's shoulders and they decided to call it an early night.

"What time do you plan on loading the Jeep in the morning?" Liz asked as they walked back into the apartment complex.

"I'd like to be on the road no later than seven," Cam replied.

"We'll be here at six to help you get loaded and to say goodbye, if that's okay?"

"Thanks, with the four of us loading it won't take long."

"Good night, you two. See you in the morning," Ruth said as she and Liz disappeared down the hall.

"Ready for bed?" Tab asked as they entered the apartment.

"Yes, I'm emotionally drained," she admitted.

"I can understand that. Let's get undressed and I'll hold you until we fall asleep."

"Thanks, Tab." Cam kissed her sweetly, then undressed.

†

By six thirty, they had the Jeep loaded.

"One last meal together before you head out for home?" Liz asked.

"Sure," Cam replied.

71

They walked into the nearly empty cafeteria and made their breakfast trays.

"I'm going to miss all of you terribly," Cam said as they took their seats.

"Just remember we are only a phone call away," Ruth reminded her with a smile. "Unlike these two, I only have one class in grad school next semester, so I can be there in a matter of hours."

Cam chuckled. "Be careful with your offer. I may take you up on that."

"I'll be there with bells on." She grinned.

"Now that's a sight I'd like to see." Tab chuckled and bumped her shoulder into Ruth's.

"Nope, for Cam's eyes only," Ruth fired back.

†

After breakfast, the group walked to Cam's Jeep.

"Thank you all for everything you've done to make me feel so welcome here," Cam told them. "I'm going to miss you guys."

Liz and Ruth hugged her with tears in their eyes. "I'll keep my bells ready, waiting for your call," Ruth teased.

"Seriously, if you need us for anything, even if it's just to give you a short break, give us a call," Liz added.

"Thanks. That means the world to me."

Tab placed an arm around her shoulders. "You mean the world to us."

"Better stop or I'm going to start crying again," she warned.

"Keep in touch," Liz said and took Ruth's hand before they turned to head inside the complex.

"I will."

Cam watched her friends walk away and turned back to Tab. "I guess this is goodbye for now. I'll call later tonight if that's okay?"

"I'll be waiting. Don't forget I love you, Cam."

"I won't, and I love you too."

She pulled away from Tab, stepped toward the truck, then turned back for a final kiss.

"I'll be seeing you soon," Tab promised.

Cam's heart lodged in her throat, rendering speech impossible. She nodded and climbed in behind the wheel, then cranked the Jeep and drove away, watching Tab wave in her rearview mirror. She tossed a final wave out the window and drove for home.

†

Her dad was cutting cane when she pulled into the drive. He walked over to greet her as she brought the Jeep to a stop and killed the engine. "Welcome home, baby," he said with a painful smile.

"Where is everyone?"

"Sandy and Wanda are out fishing and the other two are helping your mama with chores. She's having a relatively good day today."

"Do you mind if I sleep out at the camp at night? I don't want to disrupt the house until it's entirely necessary. I won't go out until after supper is done and Mama is resting for the night."

"That will be fine. I'll try to get work done in plenty of time to help with what I can," he said. "That's too much of a burden for one set of shoulders."

"I'll get my stuff hauled over to the camp and be back. When did you want to talk to the girls?"

"I thought maybe after supper tonight. You may end up with one or more of them in your bed tonight."

"That's fine. I know how devastating the news is going to be for them all." Her gaze drifted to the small construction site, where a house was being framed. "What's that?"

"Buster and his friends are working on the house he and T will move into once they're married. Our house is crowded as it is. I hope as each one of y'all gets settled and starts a family, you'll live on the property."

"I don't see why not. Keep the clan growing." She smiled weakly.

"You need help moving your stuff?"

"I'll see if T or Karen can help me load it on the boat. When I've got it unloaded, you want me to help you finish?"

"I'm just about done here for the day. I'll grab some lunch and take the load to market."

"Okay, I'll see you soon, then." Cam hugged him and walked back to the Jeep.

She pulled around to the dock and walked inside to find her mama and two sisters working in the kitchen. Her mama was the first to look up and Cam saw the pain in her eyes.

"Welcome home, Cam."

"Thanks, Mama," she answered and wrapped her in a gentle embrace. "What are you ladies whipping up in here?"

"Mama made her famous chicken salad for sandwiches," T replied.

"You reckon I can borrow T for a few minutes, Mama, to help me load my stuff in the boat to take over to the camp?"

"Sure, that's not a problem. She can help you unload too. Karen and I'll finish up here. See if you can round up your other two sisters while you're out there."

"Could be hard getting Squirt off the fish," Cam teased.

Camille chuckled. "Not once she sees you. We didn't tell her you were coming home today."

"We'll be back soon, then. Dad said he was almost finished up too."

"Hurry back, then, if you expect to get a bite in."

"Yes, ma'am. You ready, T?"

"Right behind ya."

They walked out the back door and Cam wrapped an arm around T's shoulders. "How's everyone holding up?"

"Mama's having a good day. The others don't know yet, and Dad's a hot mess, but he's holding it together for us."

"And you? How are you?"

"I still can't believe this is happening to our sweet Mama. With so many evil people running around this world, why does she have to go?"

"I wish I had an answer to that. Really, I do. Do you mind riding over to the camp to help me unload?"

"No, it'll give me a good break. It's hard to try to keep smiling all the time."

"I know that feeling. Let's get a move on and then see if we can round up the other two."

†

With T's help, Cam loaded her belongings into the boat and started across the water. Nearly halfway across to the Island, she spotted Wanda and Sandy fishing, and watched as Wanda's head popped up at the sound of the boat's motor. Wanda smiled at them and motioned for them to go to the camp. Wanda shot her a thumbs-up and Cam watched them furiously reel in their lines.

"We can always use more help unloading." She grinned at T.

"That's true. How'd you accumulate all this stuff?"

"You know me, I hate to throw anything out."

"You know they call that condition hoarding," T teased.

"Tab calls me a hoarder all the time." Her heart ached as she said Tab's name.

"You okay?" T must have seen the pain on her face.

"Yeah, just a bit overwhelmed there for a minute."

"I can surely understand that. I'm sorry Mama's illness has disrupted your life."

"There's no place I'd rather be than with my family right now."

T nodded, but Cam knew her words sounded empty. When they pulled up to the dock, T stepped off the deck to tie them off. The buzzing of an engine grew louder as Wanda drove the boat toward them.

"Let's get this stuff out on the dock, so we can carry it in quickly and get back over for lunch."

"You won't get an argument from me," T said as she caught a bag Cam tossed her.

"Good, I can't wait to get my hands on some of Mama's chicken salad."

When they pulled up to the dock, Sandy raced out of the boat. "I didn't know you were coming home today," she squealed.

"I wanted to surprise you." Cam wrapped her arms around her baby sister. "Better go tie off the boat before Wanda floats back out into the bayou."

"Dang, I forgot."

Cam shook her head at Sandy. "Hurry back. You two need to help me carry this inside and then go home for lunch. Mama told us to round you two up."

"That sounds good. I'm starving and the catfish aren't biting that great today," Wanda said.

"What? Is the great white fisherwoman losing her touch?" Cam teased Sandy.

"Naw, I think they can sense a weather change coming and aren't biting."

Cam smiled and ruffled her hair. "Good Lord, when did you get so smart?"

"I had a good teacher." She grinned at Cam.

"All right, well let's get a move on before Dad and Karen beat us to the food."

They all picked up armfuls of Cam's belongings and took them to the cabin. Cam unlocked the door and waved a hand in front of her face. "Man, this place needs a good airing out. When was the last time it was opened up?"

T chuckled. "Not long after you went back to school."

"Let's drop these bags and open up some windows, then," Cam suggested. "It smells like stinky feet."

"They would be your stinky feet," Sandy reminded her.

"Nuh-uh, my feet have never smelled that bad."

Cam looked at Wanda and T for support, but all they could do was smile back at her. "Okay, let's get these windows open."

When her bags were safely inside and the windows were wide open, Cam and her sisters headed across the bayou for lunch. Sandy walked beside her as they headed from the docks toward the house.

"I'm so glad you're home. Do you want to ride with me to drop the fish at LB's, and then I can help you at the cabin?"

"That sounds like an excellent plan, if Dad doesn't need my help with anything," she answered and placed an arm around Sandy's shoulders.

"Welcome back," Camille said as they entered the kitchen. "Everyone's here so we can get started."

They took their seats around the table and after Ronny had blessed the meal, they began devouring sandwiches and chips.

"Do you need my help with anything after lunch?" Cam asked him.

"No, honey, I think I'm calling it a day. I'll run the cane to town and come back for a nice cool shower."

"I'll help Sandy and Wanda deliver the fish, and get settled in at the camp, then. Do you need help with dinner, Mama?"

"Nope, Karen is preparing spaghetti and garlic toast. We already have a salad chilling in the refrigerator. You get settled and come over around six, and we'll be ready to eat."

"Yes, ma'am." Cam bit into a sandwich and thought about the conversation they would have after dinner. She dreaded the impact the news was going to have on her sisters. Cam wished she could do something to soften the blow.

✝

"Are you two ready to go?"

Sandy finished her tea and looked at Wanda. "Looks that way to me."

"We'll see you later, Mama. Thanks for a great lunch." Cam bent down and kissed her mama's cheek.

"Y'all be safe and don't get lost over on that Island."

Cam chuckled. "Yes, ma'am."

The three sisters emerged from the house headed for the docks. A low rumbling of thunder in the distance made Cam gaze out across the water. "We'd better get a move on before this storm catches us."

Wanda pulled the keys out of her pocket and offered them to Cam. "Oh, heck no, this is your gig now. I'm just along for the ride."

Wanda grinned and started the motor as Cam untied the line and stepped into the boat. She had barely taken her seat when Wanda pressed the throttle and the boat moved forward.

After a ten-minute ride, she pulled them into the docks at LB's and Tony met them to unload.

"Well hello, stranger," he called out when he saw Cam in the boat. "When did you get home?"

"Just this morning."

"I'm sorry to hear about your mama," he blurted out.

Cam shook her head quickly to stop him from saying more as he turned scarlet.

"What about Mama?" Sandy asked.

"It's something we'll talk about later. Now let's get these cats unloaded before that storm hits."

She looked at Tony, who mouthed, "I'm sorry." She nodded and went to work helping her sisters.

He weighed their catch and handed Wanda the receipt. "Keep bringing them in as much as you can. I know they're starting to slow down a bit, but these fish are so much better than those farm-raised ones and they sell almost as fast as you can bring them in."

"We'll do what we can," Sandy promised.

"Let's get across to the Island," Cam told Wanda. "I have a feeling that rain's gonna be cold when it hits us."

†

The boat barreled across the water, bouncing in the waves as the winds picked up and the bayou became choppy. They pulled into the dock just as the first drops of rain fell.

"We'd better hurry or we're going to get soaked," Cam said as she tied off the boat and raced her sisters inside.

"Wanda, check the windows to make sure the rain's not blowing in, please. Sandy, can you light a couple candles?"

The girls sped into action as Cam carried in two bags and placed them on the bed. Sandy and Wanda joined her several minutes later.

"We're all good so far," Wanda announced over the tapping of the rain on the tin roof.

"Good, can you hang up these clothes while I put the rest of my things away? Squirt, will you set up my bathroom?" She handed her a box of hygiene items.

Wanda pulled hangers out of the closet and tossed them on the bed. She waited until Sandy was in the bathroom before turning to Cam with a worried look. "What did Tony mean?"

"We'll all find out tonight after supper. Mama and Dad have asked for all of us to be together."

"That doesn't sound good."

Cam couldn't hide the tears in her eyes. One slipped down her cheek before she could wipe it away. "It's not, but that's all I can say for now."

Thankfully, Wanda didn't press her for further information. Cam was seriously doubting she could hold herself together right now and knew she had to get a grip before their conversation tonight. Her parents were counting on her to be strong, and she'd be damned if she'd let them down.

"Will Tab be coming down for Christmas?"

"She'll be here before Christmas but will have to go back to Monroe to celebrate with her family."

"We are her family," Wanda said. "I may be out of line, but I think she'd much rather be here."

"As usual, little sister, you are spot-on. Tab would much prefer to be here to celebrate with us, but her mother insists she be there for the holidays."

"Well, at least she'll get to spend some of it with us."

"That she will."

Sandy emerged from the bathroom holding up a scrunched tube of toothpaste. "You seriously need some toothpaste, Cam."

"I need to make a store run tomorrow. Will you grab a pen and paper to make a list for me?"

"No problem, I'll be right back." She disappeared back into the bathroom, then walked down the hall to the living room for a notepad and paper. "Number one, toothpaste." She chuckled.

"Better add some toilet paper, milk, cereal, bread, eggs, and butter too," Cam replied. "I'll be coming over for meals, but I gotta have something when I wake up hungry in the middle of the night."

"I peeked in the fridge and there's not much there. Better add some teabags, sugar, and coffee," Wanda said. "Beer too."

"Now we're talking." Cam tossed her a pair of jeans to place on the hanger.

†

When they finished unpacking, the rain had let up and they dashed for the boat and raced across the bayou. The skies opened up once more when they were walking toward the house, so they scurried inside before they got soaked.

"I see y'all brought the rain with you," Camille said from the kitchen.

"We just did make it back before it arrived in full force," Wanda said.

Cam was shocked at how her mama's appearance had changed in the few hours they were gone. She looked pale and weak, and dark circles had formed around her eyes. Cam couldn't begin to fathom the struggle her mama must be experiencing, trying to conceal her illness from her children. "Go rest until its ready, Mama. We'll set the table and help Karen. I see she hasn't burned down the kitchen yet."

"No, I haven't, smarty-pants," Karen growled from the kitchen, then rushed back to check the garlic bread in the oven.

"Take Mama and Dad a glass of tea, please Sandy, while Wanda and I set the table."

"I'll pour glasses for the rest of us," T volunteered.

"You got it smelling good in here, Karen."

Karen smiled back at Cam. "Thanks, I hope it tastes half as good as it smells. Making the sauce from scratch is a lot harder than pouring it out of a bottle."

"That's true, but it doesn't taste near as good as Mama's special recipe," Cam reminded her. Her comment made her wonder how many of her mama's recipes were in danger of being lost. She made a mental note to have Sandy in charge of working with her mama to write them down. It would give them some special time together and would ensure her recipes stayed in the family as something to remember her by. "Better check that garlic bread," Cam teased. "I smell smoke."

Karen opened the oven door to reveal the golden-brown slices of bread. "Hush, Cam, they are just now perfect."

Cam reached over Karen's head and pulled down a large platter. "Here, you can use this."

Cam retrieved the bowl of salad and dressings from the refrigerator and carried them to the table, while T brought the garlic bread. Karen strained the spaghetti, placed it in a serving bowl, and handed it to Cam.

"I'll pour up the sauce and we'll be all set. Sandy, will you get Mama and Dad?" Karen asked.

Cam looked at the meal on the table. "You did good."

"Thanks."

"I'm going to put a pot of coffee on while everyone gets settled," Cam said as Sandy returned with their parents in tow.

"This looks fantastic," Camille told Karen. "You did a lovely job with the meal."

Ronny chimed in. "It sure smells wonderful."

When they were seated around the table, they joined hands and Ronny blessed the food. "Let's dig in." He smiled and took a slice of bread before passing the platter.

The meal was fantastic, but her parents didn't seem to have much of an appetite.

Cam took another slice of bread and looked at her mama. "You know, Mama, I was thinking."

"That must have been painful," T teased.

"T, behave," her mama chided with a smile. "What were you thinking, Cam?"

"Now that everyone is out of school for a few weeks, I think it would be a good time for you and Sandy to sit down together and start writing down all your wonderful recipes."

Sandy's head popped up. "Could we, Mama?"

Camille smiled at her youngest. "I'd love to do that with you, and that is a great idea. I may have to concentrate really hard to remember some of the ingredients, though."

"No problem, Mama. I'll use pencil until we're sure, and then I'll copy them in ink."

Ronny shot Cam a smile to show his approval.

"Someone better write them down or poor Buster is going to starve to death when he and T get married," Karen snickered.

"Hey now, I can cook," T growled.

Cam smiled. "I hear Buster's a pretty fair cook, so maybe they won't starve."

"We can always come over here for some of Mama's cooking," T said.

A flash of recognition and pain crossed T's face. She must have realized that her mama probably wouldn't live to see them married.

"It's probably a good thing he'll be working on the rigs two weeks at a time. He'll eat good there." Cam elbowed her sister.

"It'll sure save on grocery bills," Ronny added. "That boy can eat."

"Yes, he can," T agreed.

Cam swallowed. "Did I hear someone say they were going to start framing the house now that the pilings were all set?"

T smiled at Cam, as if thankful for a change of subject. "Yes, Buster, his brother Jeffrey, and some friends will be out this weekend to start on it."

Cam sighed without thinking. "One day, I'll have to start building a place of my own here."

Ronny smiled. "Do you still want a spot close to the docks? You know it will need to be higher there, right?"

"I know, but that's always been my choice of spots."

"You've got a nice little nest egg built up from our 'shine business. You could get someone to build it for you," her dad suggested.

"Maybe later. Right now, I'm perfectly content at the camp."

"We haven't been doing any overnight hunts lately, so it's yours as long as you want it," Ronny said.

The meal was winding down, and Cam could sense the anxiety growing in her parents. "Girls, let's pitch in and get this table cleared and the kitchen cleaned while Mama and Dad have a cup of coffee. Then we need to sit down and have a family discussion."

Ronny looked up at her, and Cam could see his relief that she had made the dreaded announcement.

"Wanda, will you pour the coffee while we clear the table?"

"Sure. Thanks for a great meal, Karen."

"Yes, thank you. That was delicious. What are you cooking tomorrow?" Cam asked.

"It's T's turn to take over the kitchen. I think she's cooking chicken 'n' dumplings."

"You go, girl," Cam said and offered T a high five.

T slapped her palm. "You better wait until after you try them."

"You can do this," Camille said in a soft voice.

"Yes, you can," Cam agreed.

CHAPTER SIX

When everyone had finished their chores and settled around the table, Ronny cleared his throat and took a sip of his coffee. With pain in his eyes, he looked at her for support. "Your mama and I have some bad news to share, and we wanted everyone to be together for this."

Cam watched him struggle, the words choking him with emotion. He bit his lip in an attempt to hold back his tears. Until her mama's illness, she had never seen her dad cry and she reached over to place a comforting hand on his shoulder. "May I help?"

Ronny nodded.

"If you haven't noticed, Mama hasn't been feeling all that great for the last couple of months," Cam said as she looked from one terrified face to the next. "What Mama has is cancer, and it's grown to the point where it can't be treated. She and Dad saw a specialist in Baton Rouge who confirmed that there was nothing that could be done. She's in God's hands now."

Cam gave the girls a few minutes for the words to sink in before she continued. "I've come home to be with Mama and help out around here as much as I can, so I'll be asking each one of you to step up and do more."

"Oh Mama, I'm so sorry, I had no idea," Karen said.

Next to Cam, Sandy broke down crying. Cam scooped her up and pulled her into her lap, holding her close.

Ronny looked at his girls. "I know this is tough news for us to share with you, but I want you all to know how much I love you and how proud I am of each and every one of you. I want our time together to be as special as we can make it, but it has to start with the truth of the matter."

Camille took a deep breath and reached for Ronny's hand. "The doctor has told us I only have a few months left, and I want to spend as many of those days with you as I can. I'm on medications to help ease the pain, and I wish to stay in our home until my family can no longer care for me. I do not wish to be a burden on any of you, but I cannot bear the thought of being away from here until it is completely necessary."

Wanda brushed back her tears. "So, there's no hope of a miracle?"

"There's always hope for a miracle, but I'm ready to be called home. I don't want to leave my beautiful family, but when it's time, I will go in peace."

T looked at Ronny, then Camille. "What can we do?"

"As the disease worsens, I won't be able to do as much around here. I hope I won't become bedridden for quite a while yet so I'll be able to share with you what needs to be done daily. Cam will be here during the day to help your dad with running the businesses, but it's going to be important that you all help out around the house, cooking and keeping it in shape."

"You don't need to worry, Mama, we'll take care of everything," Cam promised. "You just rest and try to conserve your strength and tell us what to do if we stray." She forced herself to smile.

"I know this is asking a lot of you girls, especially you, Cam. I feel horrible for asking you to come home from school, but we didn't have any other choice."

"There is no place I'd rather be. Family always comes first in our world, and it will always be that way."

"Just promise me you'll finish school and return to playing ball once things are settled."

Cam nodded, but she knew she couldn't make that promise.

"My wish is for life to go on as much as normal as possible. Sandy and Wanda, you should continue to fish whenever you can. Teresa, we still have much work to do planning your wedding, and you all need to continue to study hard, and make good grades."

Sandy lifted her head from Cam's shoulder and looked at her mama. "I love you, Mama, and I don't want you to go."

Camille cocked her head at her baby. "Trust me, sweetheart, I don't want to leave you, but I'll be watching you from heaven after I'm gone."

"Do y'all have any other questions? Your mama is getting tired and I'd like her to go to bed now," Ronny said. "It's been a hard day for her, for all of us."

"I'm sure we'll have plenty to ask later. If it's okay, I'd like to take the girls to the camp for a bit to discuss a few things," Cam said.

"That's fine. I'll get your mama comfortable and we'll see you in the morning."

The girls kissed and hugged their parents, then followed Cam, out to the boats.

T drove a second boat to take her sisters back from the Island, and the faces and moods of the St. Angelo girls were somber as they crossed the water.

Cam had everyone sit at the table after they arrived. "I know this news absolutely sucks for the family, but Mama and Dad need us to work together now more than ever. As Mama said, I'll help Dad with the businesses and with Mama's care, but we'll need everyone to work together to keep meals coming and the house in shape."

She looked at her sisters and there wasn't a dry eye in the room. "It's going to be hard on all of us, especially Dad. They've been in love since they were your age, Squirt. That's a long time."

"I guess I didn't think of that," Wanda admitted. "I'm sorry about you having to come home from school and all."

Cam knew that the "and all" meant Tab. Even at her young age, Wanda knew the pain and impossibilities of a long-distance romance, even though Baton Rouge wasn't nearly as far as Indiana.

"It is what it is. I'd gladly give up college and softball forever if it meant Mama wasn't sick. Besides, someone's got to be around to keep you clowns out of trouble." She took a deep breath. "You heard what Mama wants us to do. Keep on keeping on, so you two try to fish everyday possible. T, you can keep Mama's mind busy planning for the wedding, and Sandy, you have recipes to write up."

"What can Wanda and I do?" Karen asked.

"Keep the house running. I may need Wanda or Sandy's help with Dad to do some of the outdoor chores. If you can keep us fed and in clean clothes that would be a great help. Especially once school starts again. I'll take over the house and caring for Mama then, while Dad does the outside stuff."

"Should I quit basketball?"

"Absolutely not, Wanda. I know Mama would enjoy attending some of your games to get her out of the house and she wouldn't want you to give it up."

"But you did, Cam."

"My situation is totally different. I'm the oldest and that comes with a lot of responsibility. I'll go back to school, when and if I can, but right now, my family needs me."

Sandy crawled up in Cam's lap, searching for comfort. "Can I stay out here tonight?"

"Of course; you can anytime. I'll be staying out here at night for a while until I'm needed at the house at night for Mama."

T fought back her tears. "Do you have any idea how bad it's going to be for her?"

"From what research I was able to do in a short time, I know it's going to be painful. The doctor has her on pain medication now, and he will continue to increase the dose or change medications depending on how she feels. Mama's a fighter. She will probably not want to take them even though she's in pain, because she doesn't want to miss a minute with us. It's important one of us is with her at all times right now."

Karen nodded. "What do we need to watch out for?"

"Mama falling, or dizziness that could cause her to fall and hurt herself. As long as she's able, she'll need to walk as much as she can tolerate. Sitting up in her recliner would be good too, while you talk about recipes or fold clothes together. She needs a reason besides us to fight."

"I saw some index cards in your boxes. Can I have those to start the recipes with Mama?"

"That would be perfect, Squirt. You can do those in the morning while Karen cooks breakfast, and you can help her with the laundry by folding it while talking with Mama. If she wants to start out writing them, then let her."

"There's fortysomething years of recipes in her head, so there will be plenty to write," Karen said and ruffled Sandy's hair.

"Is there anything we can do for Dad?" T asked.

"Give them time together at night when they want it. After supper, we can catch up on house chores and give them time."

Karen looked to Cam. "I know this is still a few weeks away, but what can we do special for her for Christmas?"

"I think we need to fill every day with something special for her. She loved to bake cookies and Christmas fudge. She always cooked the big holiday meals, so we'll need to do that under her guidance. I think we can manage a Turducken roll and I'd like to deep-fry a couple turkey breasts."

"Buster will be home from the oil fields and can help you with those," T offered. "He could probably bring up some fresh shrimp to have a boil. Maybe Christmas Eve?"

Cam smiled. "That sounds like a good plan. I think in general if Mama says she wants something, we should do everything in our power to make it happen."

"Do you think we should move up the wedding?"

"I can't answer that. You'll have to talk to Mama and Dad." The clock in the kitchen chimed. "It's getting late. Y'all better get across the water before it gets much later. Karen, are you good for starting breakfast in the morning? I know Mama will want everyone to go to church."

"I'll help her, and we'll have it ready by eight," T replied. "Biscuits, eggs, bacon, and the works."

"Squirt and I will be over early too. I think Dad is caught up on chores until Monday, so we can have a relaxing family day after church. There's one other thing. If Mama insists she wants to help, let her. She'll know if she's up to doing something and won't want to be babied."

Wanda chuckled. "I can't imagine Mama ever wanting to be babied."

Cam knew there might be a time when Camille may become incontinent or need her food to be the texture of baby food, but she refrained from speaking of it to the girls. They'd already had enough of a shock for the day. She and Sandy walked out to the boat with them. "Call me to let me know you made it home safely."

"Yes, Mama." Karen grinned.

"Be safe and don't run into anything on your way home."

She and Sandy watched them disappear into the thick night.

"It's been a long day, Squirt. I don't know about you, but I'm ready for bed."

"Can I sleep with you tonight, Cam?"

"Of course you can."

Cam slipped her arm around Sandy's shoulder and they walked inside. "Do you need one of my T-shirts to sleep in?"

"Yeah, that would be great."

"Do you still have a toothbrush over here?"

"I do. I'll brush up and come crawl in bed with you in a minute."

Cam walked into the bedroom and looked at her phone. She had missed two calls from Tab. She looked at the clock and decided it was too late to call and walked into the bathroom to prepare for bed. She had just finished brushing when her phone rang. It was Karen calling to let her know they'd made it home. "See you in the morning. Love you too," Cam told her.

She washed her face and was setting the alarm when Sandy returned. "Pick out a shirt and come climb into bed." Cam pulled back the covers and slipped into the comfortable bed. "Man, this feels good."

When Sandy climbed in, she turned out the light and snuggled in close to Cam. Cam enjoyed the closeness of her little sister and admitted she needed the comfort of a warm body next to her tonight. She was relaxed and drifting off to sleep when Sandy whispered, "Cam, after Mama is gone, will you be my mama?"

Cam's heart lodged in her throat. She wasn't expecting this question so soon. "I could never replace Mama for any of us, but I will do everything I can to be the best big sister and friend I can for all of you."

"You already do that, but I understand what you're saying."

Cam wrapped an arm around Sandy and held her close until they drifted off to sleep.

†

The next two weeks flew by in a flurry of activity. The days seemed too short to get everything accomplished they had planned for each day. After supper, Cam would drive over to the camp and collapse onto the bed, emotionally and physically exhausted. She knew her mama was fighting hard to stay active, but every day Cam sensed her weakness growing. The house filled daily with the aroma of baked goods, and their recipe project was coming along well. Cam had to buy more cards on a trip to town for groceries and found a nice wooden recipe box for Sandy to put them inside. She stayed so busy, she had lost track of Tab coming down over the weekend until Wanda reminded her. They had talked over the phone several times that week, but Cam had been so tired she had trouble focusing on any conversation. She and Ronny had cooked twice that week, getting their regular customers set for the holidays, so she was literally burning the candle from both ends.

Cam had managed to squeeze in some time to shop for Christmas presents for Tab and the rest of the family, so at least that was finished. Ronny was delivering an order of 'shine near the Texas border, so Cam had a brief respite and decided to spend it with her mama until Tab arrived later in the day. The rest of the girls would go into town to finish up their shopping and pick up the last of the groceries they needed.

†

Much to her mother's chagrin, Tab left early that morning to drive to Lake Charles to pick up Cam's Christmas present. She had struggled with the decision and finally ended up calling Ronny for his advice and blessing. She looked over at the passenger seat and smiled as she hoped Cam would when she saw her gift. It would add slightly to her workload, but she hoped Cam would appreciate the gesture as much as she was sure Sandy and Wanda would. An hour away from the bayou, she stopped for a break, then drove hard to get to her love.

†

Camille sat in her recliner as she and Cam shared a cup of coffee. "The house seems so quiet without the rest of the family."

"Yes, it does," Cam agreed. "How are you feeling today?"

"I'm having a good day. The pain is tolerable, and I managed to keep breakfast down."

The nausea had arrived with a vengeance, and Camille had begun to lose weight.

"Can I get you some of the cookies Wanda and Sandy made yesterday?"

"Maybe later. Are you excited about Tab arriving today?"

"I had almost forgotten she was coming until Wanda reminded me. Time has slipped by so quickly."

"I hope you will spend as much time with her as you can. I know she's very special to you. I'm sorry my illness has put a strain on your relationship."

"Don't even think that, Mama," Cam implored. "I wouldn't miss this time with you for anything in the world."

"I know my illness has placed a huge burden on you, and your dad, but you've done a wonderful job of caring for me and supporting the family. The girls have all worked together so nicely to make sure everything is taken care of, and they have matured so much in such a short time."

"Did T ask you about moving the wedding forward?"

"She did, but I assured her that I would be smiling down on her on her special day, and that she shouldn't move the date. We've talked a good deal about married life and what she should expect. I think she and Buster will fill their home with children to give new life to the clan."

Camille's eyes filled with tears. "I understand that you probably won't marry a man and settle down to raise a bunch of kids, but no matter who you love, be happy and content with your life."

"I will, Mama. I don't yet know what my life will be, but I'll do my best to make the most of what I have."

"I fear you will be sad and lonely without Tab, once she graduates and goes off to law school, and I do hope you will find a special, forever kind of love."

"What Tab and I have shared has been special. I've come to the realization that it will end, and she will go on without me, but I'm grateful for the time we shared together. I'm sure in time there will be another who fills my life."

"Just don't let life and love pass you by. I want you to experience the joy your dad and I have shared for so many years."

"I promise. I'm still young." Cam winked at her.

"Your dad should be home soon. What should we make for lunch?"

"Is there anything in particular you would like to eat?"

"I'm thinking some of your grilled cheese sandwiches would be good. Do we still have tomatoes?"

"There are several already sliced in the fridge. Just let me know when you're ready," Cam said.

"I can wait until he gets here. Maybe Tab will be here by then too. I don't expect your sisters to return until later today."

The dryer buzzed. "I'll be right back, Mama. You need anything?"

"Nope, I'm good. Bring the clothes in here and I'll help you fold them."

"You bet," she answered and left the room.

†

Cam put away the freshly folded laundry and was refilling their coffee when she heard a vehicle approaching. She assumed it was her father's and was surprised when her mama called out, "Tab's here."

She carried the coffee into the living room and told her mama, "I'll be right back."

Cam stepped out on the porch just as Tab pulled up in the drive. She turned off the engine and smiled as Cam approached.

The windows were down in the car, and as Cam walked toward it, a head popped up from the passenger's seat. Cam was startled for a second before she realized Tab had brought a puppy, and not just any puppy, but a Catahoula. Mostly tan with darker brown and black spots, the puppy wiggled when she saw Cam.

"Who is this?"

"This, my love, is Willow, your Christmas present. I hope you like her."

Cam reached inside and lifted out the tiny pup. "She's beautiful. Where did you find her?"

"I drove to Lake Charles early this morning to pick her up." Tab exited the car and walked around to Cam for a hug and a kiss. "I know she'll be more work for you until she's trained, but she'll be great company for you and a good addition to the family. I talked to your dad and he approved."

"You're a sneaky one, Tab Fortner. She's perfect, though."

"You might want to let her down so she can go to the bathroom."

Cam set the puppy on the ground and she walked away to find a spot to empty her bladder. "Willow, huh?"

"That's what I named her, but you can change it if you don't like it."

"It's perfect. She'll be a breeze to train. This breed is so smart and they make great companions."

"I thought you and the girls could use a bundle of energy right now."

"Sandy and Wanda are going to be thrilled. Thanks, Tab."

"How's your mama?"

"Having a good day. We're having coffee. Would you like some?"

"Yes, but after a bathroom break of my own."

"Come on, let's go inside, then. Come, Willow." Cam's face lit up with a smile as the puppy rushed back to her. "Good girl." Cam picked her up and reached for Tab's hand as they walked to the house.

"Oh my, would you look at this." Camille reached for the puppy when Tab and Cam entered. "Who is this?"

"Your newest daughter, Willow," Cam explained. "She's my Christmas present from Tab."

"Your dad mentioned a puppy. She's beautiful."

Cam smiled as Willow climbed into her mama's lap and began licking her face. "She seems right at home."

"Well aren't you just the sweetest thing," Camille cooed to the puppy.

"Take your bathroom break and I'll pour you a cup of coffee," Cam told Tab.

"I'm sorry, Tab. It's good to see you too, honey. I got sidetracked by this little girl."

Tab leaned down and kissed Camille's cheek. "It's good to be here. I'll be right back."

Cam poured the coffee and watched her mama play with Willow. The puppy was performing her magic. Camille was laughing as Willow licked her face and wiggled in her lap. Seeing her mama so happy was worth everything. She picked up the cup and walked back into the living room.

"Do you want me to take her?"

"Heavens no, she's such a bundle of joy. She'll settle down in a minute after she's greeted me properly."

Cam smiled and sat next to her. "She is a cutie."

"Such a perfect gift for you," Camille said as she stroked the pup's soft coat as Willow curled up in her lap. "They stay small, don't they?"

"Yes, they do, about two feet tall at best."

Tab walked back into the room. "The breeder said she was the runt of the litter, so I'm not sure she'll reach full height."

"The runt is usually the best dog of the bunch, and you certainly seemed to pick well," Camille said.

"I think she picked me. She ran right to me and wiggled until I picked her up. After that, the other pups were of no interest to me."

Camille stroked Willow. "You can bet she'll be spoiled. The girls will go crazy for her when they get home."

Tab sat next to Cam. "Where is everyone?"

"They are in town finishing up their Christmas shopping and picking up some groceries. Dad is making a delivery but should be home soon."

"So how are you feeling?" she asked Camille.

"Better now." She smiled. "My other two daughters have arrived."

Tab smiled warmly at Camille. "Thank you. This place always feels like home to me."

"You will always be more than welcome here. I hope you know that."

"Yes, ma'am, I do. I hear we have big plans for this next week."

"I wish you could stay through Christmas, but I understand your need to be with your parents."

"I may try to sneak back for New Year's before heading back to school, if that would be all right?"

Cam looked at her. "That would be great." She turned at the sound of another vehicle arriving and saw her dad's truck pulling into the yard. "I know he's going to be hungry. I'm going to start lunch."

"Do you need my help?"

"No, stay and visit with Mama and Dad. I'm making grilled cheese with tomato sandwiches."

"That sounds yummy."

"She makes the best," Camille added.

†

Ronny walked through the door, and Cam kissed him before continuing on to the kitchen. "Welcome home, Tab," he said when he entered the living room. "And who is this?" he asked, bending down to kiss Camille and stroke the puppy.

"This, my love, is Willow, our newest addition to the family."

Willow licked his hand, and Ronny chuckled. "Yep she'll fit right in, and she's a charmer." He sat beside Tab. "You did well."

"Thanks, I'm glad she has a home here. I couldn't think of a better place to grow up than with this family."

"She's gonna be spoiled rotten, I can tell that already." He grinned at the smile on his wife's face.

"Yep, she hasn't been out of Mama's lap since she came into the house," Cam called from the kitchen.

"Imagine that." He smiled and reached over to cover Camille's hand with his.

"Did your trip go well?" she asked.

"Yes, we have some satisfied customers in Texas. Made me promise to keep the 'shine coming their way."

"That shouldn't be a problem. Cam's got a few more batches of mash brewing," Camille said.

"If you'll excuse me, I'll go see if I can set the table for Cam," Tab said and exited the room to give the couple a few minutes of privacy.

As she walked into the kitchen, she noticed that Cam looked tired. Tab couldn't begin to imagine the strain that was bearing down on her shoulders. "Can I set the table and get drinks ready?" she asked when Cam looked up from the stove to find her standing there.

"Yes, that would be great. I guess I need to round up some bowls and food for Willow too."

"Nope, I've got that covered. Two sets of bowls, one for here, and another for the camp, two bags of puppy food, a leash, and a bed. Somehow, I doubt she'll be spending much time in the bed, though, but she'll have it anyhow."

"You thought of everything, didn't you?"

"I tried. Her shots and medical treatments are all up-to-date, so she won't need anything for several months. She really seems to be taken with your mama."

"Vice versa I'd say too. Mama's eyes just light up when Willow licks her face." She chuckled. "I'll take the dog bed to the camp. I think she'll be in Mama's lap when she's here."

Tab moved around the dining room table setting plates and then walked back into the kitchen. "Tea for everyone?"

"Yes, that's the drink of choice these days."

"I'll go ahead and pour them and grab the bowls and food for Willow so she won't be begging from the table."

Cam looked up from the stove. "Thank you for such a precious gift."

"I was hoping she'd keep you company when I can't be with you."

"I just hope she's not a bed hog."

Tab placed the filled glasses on the table. "I'll be right back."

She glanced into the living room on her way down the hall and saw Cam's parents playing with Willow, confirming she had made a good choice. As she walked out to her car, she spotted T's car coming down the drive. Apparently, the girls had finished their shopping early. She took a set of the bowls and a small bag of puppy food from her backseat and waited for T to pull up.

Sandy was the first to emerge from the car. "What's the puppy food and bowls for?" she asked, looking puzzled as she approached Tab.

"Cam's Christmas present. I brought her a puppy."

Sandy's face lit up. "Really? Where is it?"

"I do believe your mama is spoiling her rotten."

"Cool. Good to see you, Tab," she said and raced into the house.

Wanda and the rest began pulling out bags to carry inside. "Did y'all have lunch yet?" Tab asked.

"Not yet, we wanted to get home," Wanda answered.

"I'll tell Cam to cook more sandwiches, then." Tab took a few bags from her and walked inside.

Sandy was kneeling in front of her mama, receiving a good face licking from Willow. It was good to hear laughter in the house. She imagined there hadn't been much to laugh about in the weeks since Camille's diagnosis, but she hoped to change that, if even for a short while. She continued on to the kitchen. "The crew is home, so you'd better add more sandwiches. They haven't had lunch yet."

"What's that noise?" Cam asked.

"Your baby sister is drowning in kisses from Willow and enjoying every second. Her giggles are contagious."

"That's a very good thing. I hope to be drowning in kisses later too."

"I'll talk to Willow and see what we can do," Tab teased.

"Okay, smarty-pants, better add plates and tea to the table while I get cooking."

Cam pulled out a second frying pan to double the sandwich production as the crew filed in carrying bags of presents and groceries. "You'll need to put those away while I fix lunch," she instructed Karen.

Tab walked into the kitchen from the dining area. "Okay, the table is set, what else can I do?"

"Go ahead and get our parents in here, and y'all eat before the sandwiches get cold," Cam told Tab.

Tab called Ronny and Camille into the kitchen. "Sandy, will you take Willow outside while I get her food together?"

"Sure, Tab," she called out and ran out the front door with Willow hot on her heels.

"Go ahead and eat, and I'll get the food and water out," Wanda offered. "She's a beauty, by the way."

Tab handed Wanda the bowls and sat down beside Camille at the table. "This looks delicious."

"She makes the best grilled cheese," Camille said.

"I had a great teacher, and lots of practice," Cam replied.

"That's true." Ronny bit into his sandwich, emitting a soft moan. "I sure hope there's a second with my name on it."

"I'll make you as many as you can eat," Cam promised as she handed two more plates of sandwiches to T and Karen, then turned to start making more.

Wanda filled the bowl half-full of ice cubes and then cold water.

"That's right, go ahead and spoil my puppy rotten," Cam teased.

"It's hot outside." Wanda grinned back at her as she placed the ice water beside the food bowl.

The screen door opened and Sandy came in with Willow trotting beside her. "Show her where her food and water are, please," Cam said, waving the spatula in the air for emphasis.

Sandy chuckled at her antics. "You got it. Come on, Willow."

"Dad, are you ready for another?"

"I will be by the time you get it cooked. You need to sit down and eat too."

"In just a few minutes I will. Does anyone else want seconds? Mama?"

"No, honey, I'm good with one."

"Will you split one with me?" Karen asked T.

"Sure thing."

"Karen, please bring me your and Dad's plates," Cam said and cut one of the sandwiches in two.

She placed two more sandwiches on to cook and put them on her plate when they were done. "Last call?"

When no one answered, Sandy looked at Cam. "I'll split that one with you."

Cam cut the sandwich in half and gave one to Sandy, then took a bite. "Damn, I am good," she crowed. "There's enough left for extras." She looked at Tab.

"Not me, I'm saving room for the brownies over there." Tab nodded to the plate sitting on the counter.

"I forgot all about those," Ronny sighed.

"Keep on forgetting about them. That leaves more for me," Sandy said as she leaned over and bumped into his shoulder.

Ronny smiled at his baby. "Since y'all finished shopping early, do you plan to fish today?"

Sandy looked at Wanda. "We hadn't planned to, but we can."

"If Cam will help me, I think it's time we have a fish fry. Would you like that, Mama?" he asked.

"I can never turn down fresh catfish and Cam's hush puppies," she answered.

Sandy whipped her head around to look at Tab. "You up for some fishing?"

Tab looked over to Cam, who nodded. "Sure, I'd like that. I gotta keep my fishing skills intact."

"Will you make some Creole coleslaw, Wanda?" Cam asked. "We have peanuts."

"That does sound good, with hush puppies and corn on the cob," Ronny said. "Man, how can I be hungry again already?"

"It's just the suggestion of food." Camille smiled at him. "If y'all don't mind, I think I'll lie down for a bit."

Wanda stood from the table. "You need some help?"

"No, I'm good, but thanks. Y'all have fun fishing. Don't let me sleep the day away," she told Ronny.

"Two hours plenty?" he asked.

"That should be." She stood slowly and walked to the master bedroom.

Willow ate a good portion of the food Wanda put out for her, then walked over to sit on the floor beside Cam.

"Was that good, pretty girl?"

Willow licked her lips and walked back over for a long drink. Sandy had finished eating. "Would you mind taking her back outside for me?" Cam asked.

"Under one condition."

"We have conditions now?" Cam chuckled. "Dare I ask?"

"I'll take her out if you'll let Willow go fishing with us."

"Well, she's certainly going to have to learn to ride in a boat if she's going to live here, so why not? Just don't let her fall out. She wouldn't even be a snack for Bubba Gump."

Sandy beamed. "I promise I'll take good care of her."

"See, what did I tell ya? They're spoiling her rotten," she said to Tab.

†

Cam finished cleaning the kitchen while Ronny set up the cookers for the fish fry.

"Why don't we relax for a little while, and then once your mama is up we can start on dinner?"

"Can you and Wanda handle skinning the cats?"

"I think we can manage that while you get started on the inside work."

"I just hope our great white fisherwomen don't come back with a well full of fish," Cam replied.

"If they do, I'll pick us out a mess and they can take the rest to LB's."

"That sounds like a good plan."

†

Cam kicked back in a recliner while T and Karen disappeared to their bedrooms and Ronny went to check on Camille. Her eyes grew heavy, and the next thing she knew, T was shaking her awake.

"Wake up, sleeping beauty; it's time to start dinner."

"Is Mama up yet?"

"Yep, she's enjoying the sunshine with Dad."

"Are the fisherwomen back yet?"

"Nope, but they probably won't be out much longer."

Cam stood and stretched. "I see Karen's already working on the slaw. Do you mind chopping a few onions for me while I get the hush-puppy mix started?"

"Not at all. Do you want me to cook the corn inside while y'all do the frying outside?"

"That would be a huge help."

Cam had just finished preparing the batter for the hushpuppies when Ronny came inside carrying a pan full of filets.

"Will one of you soak these in buttermilk until they're ready to be cooked?"

"No problem." T took the pan of fish from him. "Where are the girls?"

"Making a run over to LB's. There's no way we could eat all the fish they caught. I swear those sisters of yours are fish magnets." He chuckled and turned to go outside. "Oh, and Willow is sound asleep in your mama's lap. I think the boat ride and fresh air wore her out," he told Cam.

"I just hope she doesn't keep me up all night."

"I have a feeling Sandy will be playing with her when she gets back. I don't know which of us appreciates your Christmas present the most. Tab made an excellent choice."

"That, she did," Cam agreed.

†

The following day, Cam and Tab took Wanda into town to say farewell to Logan. It was painful to watch the two young women say goodbye, and Cam felt the heartache her sister was experiencing. When the last boxes were loaded onto the moving van, Logan's mom called for her.

"I promise I'll write," she said as she pulled away from Wanda's embrace.

Wanda nodded as the tears flowed down her cheeks, then watched as her first love got in the moving van and drove away.

Cam wrapped an arm around her shoulders. "You may not believe me now, but everything will be okay."

"I know you're right, but damn, it feels like my heart's being ripped out of my chest."

"Come on, the family will be home from church soon. Let's go get a jump on making lunch," Cam said as she turned her back toward Tab's car.

"Mama beat us to that punch. She put a huge pot roast in the Crock-Pot earlier," she reported. "We can make some other vegetables and rolls to go with it then and have everything set when they get home."

"Okay, Cam," Wanda said as she slipped into the backseat.

"You know what?" Tab said as she slid the key in the ignition.

"What?" Wanda answered.

"I never got to go snipe hunting this summer as y'all promised."

Wanda shot a grin at Cam. "We did forget, didn't we?"

Cam nodded. "You know, I heard some out the other night, pretty close to the camp. Why don't we see if Squirt wants to join us for a hunt tonight?"

"That sounds like a good plan," Wanda said, forcing a smile. "I bet Willow will be great at tracking them."

"I bet you're right," Cam agreed. "A-hunting we will go."

†

Tab had the table set and Wanda was pulling fresh-baked rolls out of the oven when the rest of the family returned. Cam was placing ears of corn in a bowl and had already dished up a massive portion of macaroni and cheese.

"My word, it smells good in here," Ronny announced. "I dreamed about that pot roast all through the preacher's sermon."

"I think half the congregation noticed you couldn't keep your eyes open," Camille replied.

"Hopefully the Good Lord will forgive me."

"You three have been busy." Camille smiled as she looked over at the table, which was set and ready for a meal.

"We thought we'd get a jump on lunch. Are you ready to eat?" Cam asked her.

"I want to change into something more comfortable."

"That's not a bad idea at all."

"It sounds like you were plenty comfortable at church, Dad," Cam teased.

"Mama had to elbow him several times to stop him snoring." Sandy snickered.

"Hey now, you don't have to tell all my business. Let's go before I get into more trouble here." Ronny smirked.

"Where's T?" Tab asked.

"She decided to stay in town, and have Sunday dinner with Buster's family," Karen said.

Wanda came back inside with Willow in tow. "Did Cam tell you we're taking Tab snipe hunting tonight?"

"No, she didn't." Sandy frowned.

"I thought maybe y'all could go fishing while I finish some chores here and we could hunt after dinner."

"It's always a good time to fish."

"You don't need my help here?" Tab asked.

"Naw, I've just got a few things to do."

†

After the meal, the family dispersed. Tab, Wanda, and Sandy went fishing, while Karen cleaned the kitchen and started laundry. Willow seemed torn between going fishing with Sandy or staying with Cam.

"Go on, you know you love riding in the boat," Cam told her.

Camille was tired and decided she and Ronny would nap for a bit. Cam went out to check on the fermenting mash in the barrels and started a new batch. There were plenty of leftovers from lunch, which they would heat for dinner, so she didn't need to do any major cooking. Cam decided she would bake after she finished her chores. She planned to make yellow cake with chocolate icing because it was her mama's favorite.

She thought about Tab and snipe hunting as she stirred the mash. She wasn't entirely sure Tab knew what it was, being a city girl, but she was thankful for the reminder to help Wanda take her mind off her heartache.

When she walked into the house, Karen was just pulling a load of sheets out of the dryer. "Let me help you with those, and then I'm going to bake Mama a cake."

"I've got these. Go get your cake started."

Cam pulled out a mix from the pantry and started gathering ingredients as she listened to the soft Zydeco music Karen had playing in the kitchen. She soon found herself swaying to the rhythm as she mixed up the batter. When the oven was preheated, she poured the batter in the pans and walked into the living room to sit in a recliner until her timer went off. By now Karen had finished folding the sheets.

"How much more laundry is there?"

"A couple loads of towels and we'll be caught up."

"Bring them in here once they're dry and I'll help you fold them."

"You just sit back and relax. I've got this. You've been running around like a crazy woman lately."

"Thanks," Cam answered and kicked her feet up.

Karen noticed how quickly Cam fell asleep and decided not to wake her when the timer went off. Cam had been working hard to keep the family and businesses running, so every chance she got; she planned to give her a break. She put the clean sheets away and waited for the cake to finish baking. She placed the pans on racks to cool and would wake Cam later, in time to ice the cake before supper. A few hours of sleep wouldn't hurt her big sister one bit.

✝

Cam had just finished icing the cake when Tab and Wanda entered the house.

"Where's Sandy?" she asked.

Tab grinned. "She's outside playing with Willow."

"How was the fishing?"

"Good according to Sandy. We delivered another seventy pounds. I also got to meet Bubba Gump today."

"Really?"

"He was sunning himself on the bank as we passed a slough. That is the biggest gator I've ever seen."

"He's big and mean."

113

"I kinda figured that. Wanda steered the boat away from him, and Sandy held on to Willow."

"I think she loves that pup as much as I do."

Tab chuckled. "Maybe more."

"She's been good therapy for all of us. I love the smile on Mama's face when she curls up in her lap."

"It's like having a baby all over again," Tab suggested.

"Yeah, one with a warm, soft tongue."

"There is that. Would you have it any other way?"

"Heck no. She's been a blessing for all of us. I've heard Sandy talking to her, and it's the sweetest thing, her explaining things to Willow."

"That's a yummy-looking cake."

"Mama's favorite." Tears flooded Cam's eyes.

"Are you all caught up in here?"

"Yes, until it's time to reheat dinner. Why?"

"I thought we might sit out in the yard and relax and watch Sandy and Willow play." Tab felt like her lover needed a distraction. "What do you say?"

"I can't say no to you. Come on. Call me if you need me, please, Karen."

"Will do," Karen called back from the living room.

Tab reached for her hand and led Cam to the backyard. They sat in large chairs around the fire pit and watched as Sandy threw a tennis ball that Willow would retrieve and drop back at her feet. Every so often, Willow would bring the ball to Sandy, but refuse to drop it until Sandy chased her laughing, until they were both tired. Sandy would collapse on the ground, and Willow would drop the ball beside her, then lie down until Sandy got up again. Watching them play warmed Tab's heart. She glanced over at Cam and saw the warmth in her smile too as she watched them. "I love you."

Cam turned her head at the sound of Tab's voice. "I love you too."

"Is there really such a thing as a snipe?"

"Yes, there is. But we really don't hunt them. It's sort of a rite of passage as a practical joke, but it's a lot of fun."

"I figured as much, the way Sandy and Wanda chuckle every time it's mentioned."

"That was a brilliant suggestion, though, to take Wanda's mind off Logan, if even for a short time."

"I thought so too." She took Cam's hand. "Will I win a prize for playing along?" She wiggled her eyebrows.

"I'll see what can be arranged on such short notice."

†

"Snipe hunting, huh?" Ronny smirked. "It's been a while since you've had one of those. Not much meat to 'em, Tab, so I hope y'all get a bunch or we'll be eating hot dogs."

"I'll do my best, sir," she replied, playing along.

Sandy giggled as she passed a slice of cake to Wanda. "This is going to be so much fun."

"Do we have any feed sacks left, Dad?" Cam asked with a straight face.

"No, but we've got an oyster sack. Will that work?"

"I'm thinking that might be perfect."

"Did you teach Tab how to make the call?" Wanda pitched in to the conversation.

Cam grinned. "I forgot all about that. Will you teach her?"

Wanda demonstrated a clucking sound, and Tab repeated it back to her. "I think you've got it. We need a few flashlights so we can drive them toward Tab."

"You can take the ones from the boats. Just be sure to put them back tomorrow," Ronny said. "Don't forget to watch out for the Rougarou."

"The what?" Tab asked.

"The Rougarou. He's the swamp monster of Louisiana. It's part man, part wolf, with burning red eyes. Whatever you do, if you run into him, don't look into those eyes."

"Stop now, Ronny St. Angelo, or your babies won't sleep tonight," Camille chastised.

"They need to know what to do if they're gonna be in da swamp after dark. Make plenty of noise so he knows you're coming," he warned.

Cam had heard the story when she was little, but Tab, Wanda, and Sandy were staring at Ronny. "Like Bubba Gump is da monster of the swamp, so is Rougarou. Bubba Gump you can see in broad daylight, but the Rougarou only travels at night, so beware." Ronny let out an evil-sounding laugh, and they jumped in their seats.

"Dad, quit teasing us," Wanda cried out.

Ronny lifted his hands in a signal of surrender. "Believe what you want, but beware."

Cam looked at Tab. "You still up for a snipe hunt?"

"Umm, yeah, I guess so. You're going to protect us, right?"

"With my life. Wanda, go get the oyster bag. We've got snipes to catch."

"I'll get the flashlights," Sandy said and left the room.

"Y'all be careful, and hopefully we'll see you for breakfast tomorrow." Ronny smiled at them.

"Good night, Mama, love you," Cam said.

"I love y'all too, honey."

"And you, dear Father, will probably have us all screaming at the slightest creak at the camp tonight. For that, I thank you." Cam hugged her dad.

"My pleasure. Good night." He smiled and took her mama to the bedroom.

†

Cam and Tab walked out to meet Sandy and Wanda for the ride back to the Island. Darkness had fallen, so Cam drove slowly across the bayou to the camp.

"That was really mean of Dad to tell us that story tonight," Wanda growled.

"It's a Cajun legend. Or is it?" Cam chuckled.

"Geez, you're as bad as your dad." Tab punched her in the arm.

"I'll go inside and get my pistol just in case we run into him."

Tab chuckled as Cam stepped off the boat to walk to the cabin.

When she returned, Cam lit the campfire. "I know Dad's story may have you a little spooked, so let's try to stay close together. We will all call for the snipes and herd them toward you, Tab, and all you have to do is catch them and put them in the bag."

"You make it sound so easy."

"I've lit the campfire as a beacon in case we get separated. If we do, don't panic, and work your way back to the scent and glow of the fire. Agreed?"

Cam looked around the small group and everyone nodded. Wanda and Sandy knew how to run a snipe hunt. They slowly peeled back until the hunter was left alone in the dark. Cam would stay close to ensure Tab's safety, and after a few minutes would explain the ruse and bring her back to the campfire to make s'mores.

"Are we all set? Wanda, you take the left flank, and Sandy take the right?" She looked at Sandy. "Keep Willow on her leash. Tab and I will proceed up the middle. Flashlights handy?"

Everyone turned on their lights as they walked slowly into the woods. "Watch your steps," Cam whispered.

Wanda and Sandy started making the calls to lure the snipe closer, and Tab followed suit. Cam followed about twenty feet behind Tab so she could keep an eye on all three.

†

Tab had to admit the absolute blackness looming ahead of the beam of her flashlight was intimidating. She trusted Cam implicitly and knew she would never put Tab or her sisters in harm's way, but Ronny's story of the Rougarou had her nerves on edge. It probably was a story told to keep kids obedient, but she knew every legend had a bit of truth to it. *Just like bigfoot.* Something had to have sparked the legend.

She made her calls, saw the beams of the girl's flashlights to each side of her, and heard their faint clicking noises. The snipe hunt was a ruse, but also a rite of passage to children living in rural areas, so she would play her part. She was thankful Cam had loaned her a pair of work boots to slog through the mushy woods. The crickets grew silent as

118

she made her way deeper into the trees, then realized the calls had grown silent.

Tab spun to the left, then to the right, but there was no sign of the girls. Her heart pounded when she realized she was alone in the dark. She stopped to ward off the rising panic, then heard a branch snapping behind her. She wheeled around, her flashlight beam flying off the ground to reveal Cam's face.

"Easy there, trigger," Cam said as she lifted her hand to block the blinding light. "It's just me."

"You scared me, Cam." Tab could hear the whimper of emotion in her voice.

"It's okay, honey. It's just the two of us now. Sandy and Wanda have probably made it back to the campfire and are giggling about the hunt." Cam pulled her into her arms and kissed her. "Have you had enough snipe hunting?"

"Yes, but I'll take another of your kisses."

Cam leaned down and kissed her sweetly with a promise of more to come. "I told the girls we'd make s'mores. Is that okay with you?"

"Of course it is, silly, but I'm ready for you to take me home now. It's way too dark out here."

Cam took her hand and led her back toward the camp. As they grew closer, Tab smelled the fire and saw the glow between the tree branches. When the camp came into view, Sandy and Wanda were sitting in chairs waiting to cook s'mores. She and Tab walked into the clearing and both girls smiled at Tab's empty bag.

"I reckon you didn't catch any," Wanda said.

"No, big goof, but it was fun. I'm ready for some s'mores, though. Snipe hunting works up an appetite."

Both girls giggled and started making s'mores, and Cam and Tab settled down in their seats to supervise the cooking. They were happily munching on their tasty treats when they heard a noise just beyond the clearing. Something big was moving through the woods, grunting and growling as it approached.

"Flashlight," Cam ordered, and Sandy scrambled to get hers and handed it to Cam. Cam turned the beam toward the direction of the sound and a pair of blood-red eyes shined back at them. Even the courageous Cam was startled and jumped backward. Tab had been holding Willow in her lap and was surprised when the pup started growling and the hackles stood up along her spine.

"What is it, Cam?"

"I don't know." Cam slipped her pistol out of the holster and took several cautious steps forward. "You and the girls stay back," she instructed. "Hang on tight to Willow."

"I've got her," Tab replied.

Her light caught the flash of red eyes once more, and as she moved toward them, it revealed the source of the glowing eyes, and Cam released the breath she was holding. A very pregnant wild sow was rooting around the feeder looking for an easy meal. When she realized Cam was coming toward her, she let out an ungodly squeal and fled, crashing through the woods.

"Cam, is everything all right?" Tab called.

Cam turned and strolled back toward the fire. "Too much Rougarou talk tonight. It was a wild sow looking for an easy meal. One good look at me and she ran squealing into the woods."

They let out breaths of relief and returned to their seats around the campfire as the fire began to burn low. Cam decided against adding more wood, as they had all had enough excitement for the day. "I think it's time to call it a night. Thanks for snipe-hunting with us."

"It was a bit scary, but fun," Tab admitted.

"Can you two put the fire out?" Cam asked her sisters.

Wanda nodded. "Yeah, I think we can handle that. We won't be far behind ya."

†

"It was quite an exciting night, wasn't it?" Tab slowly peeled off her T-shirt.

Cam admired the view and forgot Tab had asked a question until Tab smiled at her. "Yes, it was. I admit that sow gave me a scare. I think Dad had us on all edge with his story."

"That was cruel, but I'm betting he'll get a good laugh when he hears the story."

"I'm sure he will. But now I'm ready for a different kind of excitement," she said as she stepped forward and took Tab in her arms. "I bet you're just the right woman to provide it too."

"I would certainly hope so."

Their upper bodies were naked, and Cam enjoyed the feel of Tab's soft, warm skin pressed into hers as she leaned down for a kiss. Tab moaned softly, causing Cam to break the kiss with a smile.

"Don't forget we have two sisters in the bedroom next door, and these walls aren't incredibly thick."

"So no screaming out your name in my throes of passion?" Tab asked.

"Not tonight, I'm afraid. Should I find something to gag you? A sock maybe?"

"Eww, Cam St. Angelo, don't even think it," Tab warned. "Talk about a buzzkill."

Cam kissed down to Tab's neck. "I think I can get that buzz started again," she whispered in her ear, then wrapped her lips around Tab's earlobe.

"That's a good start, but you'll have to work harder than that."

"I have no problem with hard work," Cam answered as she unfastened Tab's jeans and slid them and her panties to the floor.

Tab stepped out of them as she worked on Cam's jeans. "I do love that about you."

"You can work me as hard as you want, ma'am. I aim to please." Cam slid her hand between them, and brushed her fingertips across an erect nipple, stopping to deliver a soft pinch to each. She moved Tab onto the bed and climbed in beside her. She ran her hands fluidly across Tab's skin, making chill bumps rise to the surface. She knew every sensitive spot on her lover, and her touch began to weave its magic as Tab's back arched, as if begging her fingers for a firmer response. Cam replaced her touch with kisses as she moved down Tab's body to nestle between her breasts. Cam rested her thigh between Tab's and felt the wetness coating her skin as she pressed into her center and covered Tab's breast with her mouth.

Tab moaned as Cam's hair cascaded across her skin. Cam knew she was driving her wild with the gentle teasing, and she politely ignored Tab's efforts to rush her. Cam would have her way with her in due time, and the result was well worth the wait. She looked into Tab's eyes and saw the passion pooled in them, and her heart skipped a beat. Tab so easily took her breath away with a look or a sensual touch, and Cam knew she was hitting all the right spots tonight, but there was one in particular where she looked forward to arriving.

Cam had grown familiar with Tab's body and could sense her growing need for release. She caressed down Tab's front, eliciting a deeper moan of pleasure. She pulled her mouth away from sucking Tab's breast and kissed Tab's lips to conceal the gasp she would make when Cam thrust her fingers deep inside Tab's welcoming wetness. She felt the vibration inside her mouth as Tab's hips thrust off the bed, wanting more. Cam would never tire of the feeling of Tab's inner muscles grasping at her fingers as she moved them in and out of her wetness. The feeling was enough to send her arousal soaring.

Tab broke the kiss to gasp for breath as her climax tightened every muscle in her body, shutting down her diaphragm.

"Oh, hell yes, Cam," she groaned, but not too loudly.

Cam curled her fingers deep inside her, and Tab shook her head and grabbed for her wrist. "I swear if you don't stop, I'm going to scream and wake everyone in the house," she warned.

Heeding her impassioned warning, Cam slowly withdrew her fingers as Tab shuddered with pleasure.

"Did the excitement of the Rougarou bring that out of you?"

"No, silly. It was all your doing. Damn, that felt good."

"I'm glad you enjoyed it as much as I did." Cam smiled.

"You did? Really?"

"Yes. Unlike the woman I love, I can come quietly."

Tab smacked her forehead. "Damn, I thought I was being quiet. Do you think I woke them up?"

"Sandy sleeps like a log, and if Wanda was still awake, we'll know by the smile on her face in the morning."

"Oh dear, how am I to keep from blushing when I look at Wanda tomorrow?"

"Concentrate, honey, that's all you can do. Do you think you can sleep now?"

"With your body wrapped around me, heck yeah."

"Good night, then, my love."

CHAPTER SEVEN

The next morning around the breakfast table, Cam had everyone laughing heartily at the adventure with the snipe hunt, and the faux-Rougarou sighting.

"I can just imagine your reaction when those red eyes were shining back at you," Ronny said.

"I've never been so close to peeing on myself my entire adult life," Cam admitted. "I've never heard the likes of the sounds she was making."

"She probably smelled the sweet odor of your s'mores," Camille replied.

"You think so?"

"Trust me, when you're pregnant, all of your senses are heightened, especially smell, both good and bad. As much as I love gingerbread cookies, I couldn't stand to smell them when I was pregnant with you, Cam." She looked around the room. "Then when Teresa came along, I couldn't get enough mint–chocolate-chip ice cream."

"Now dat's the truth. I bet I made twenty trips to town for ice cream," Ronny added.

"No wonder it's my favorite," T replied.

"What about me, Mama?" Karen asked.

Ronny chuckled. "Oh, I remember that one. It was mudbugs, and thanks be to the Good Lord we had some frozen in the freezer."

Camille's gaze landed on Wanda. "Now yours was by far the weirdest."

"How so?"

"Bread-and-butter pickles with yellow mustard." She broke out laughing. "If your poor dad didn't have a plate for me when I first woke up, I'd be sicker than a dog."

"It didn't take us long to figure that one out." Ronny scrunched up his face and held his nose.

Camille smiled at Sandy. "And you, my sweet baby girl. You wanted fresh strawberries and whipped cream several times a day."

"I still love them." Sandy smiled and crawled into her mama's lap.

"Yes, you do."

"I'm surprised it wasn't catfish, as much as you love to fish." Cam reached across to ruffle Sandy's hair.

"That would have made perfect sense," Tab agreed.

"What do you have in store for us today, Dad?" Cam asked.

"I'd like you to help me move the barrels of mash out to the camp so we can start cooking early tonight. Everything else is done for now."

"The girls and I are going to make some Christmas jelly today," Camille announced.

"Apple cinnamon?" Cam asked.

"Yes, I know it's your favorite."

"Oh, Mama, I can taste it now. It's been a few years since you made it. Tab, it's the prettiest red you can imagine."

Tab looked at Camille. "Would you mind if I helped so I can learn how to make it?"

"Of course you can. The more the merrier, right, girls?"

"Right, Mama," came the chorus of replies.

"You want to start cooking early, then, Dad?"

"Wanda, would you mind being a lookout for us and climb up in the deer stand?"

"I'd love to."

"The whole family will be cooking today, then." He shot a grin at Cam.

"I'll send T and Tab out with sandwiches later," Camille promised.

"Wonderful, my love." He stood and kissed her sweetly. "Daylight's a-wasting, Cam. Let's get a move on."

"Right behind you." She took a final sip of coffee.

"Do you want me to make you a thermos to go?" Karen asked.

"Not unless you want me wired all day."

"Trust me, that's not a pretty sight," Sandy teased.

"Hey now, you're supposed to have my back," Cam said and kissed her mama. "Let's go, Wanda."

†

Cam and Wanda followed their dad out to the shed and within minutes had five barrels of mash loaded onto the boat. Cam secured them with a strap and they drove across the water, a chill breeze blowing in her face. They rarely cooked during daylight hours, but her dad wouldn't have agreed if he thought it unsafe.

When they reached the Island, they unloaded the boat and Cam fired up the still. Ronny checked the batteries on the two-way radios and handed one to Wanda. He walked her out to the tip of their property and watched her climb safely onto the deer stand to act as their lookout.

"Call us if you see anything suspicious. I doubt you will this close to the holiday but stay sharp and let us know when lunch arrives."

"I will, Dad." Wanda was proud that he trusted her with such an important job as she climbed into her seat to begin her vigil. The stand was equipped with night-vision goggles and field binoculars. She pulled down the binoculars and scoured the surrounding area. "Not even a fisherman," she said.

†

Cam had dropped the first load of mash into the cooker and was mixing up the paste to seal the joints when Ronny returned. "Is Wanda in place?"

"Yes, she is. She was already scanning when I turned to look back."

"She's an eagle eye for sure."

"You want to start labeling our bottles while I seal the joints?" he asked. "Your handwriting is so much better than mine."

"You got it." She handed him the container of paste, walked over to a small cabinet that held the labels she would use, and pulled them out, along with a permanent marker. She returned to a folding lawn chair and began making the labels. "Are you planning to make another delivery run this week?"

"I thought I'd go ahead and make a delivery to Baton Rouge, and a few of our locals have asked for a delivery as well."

"Do you want me to handle those while you go to Baton Rouge?"

"Thanks, honey, but I'd feel more comfortable doing them myself. I can't risk anything happening to you right now." He finished the last seal and took a seat beside her as he watched the cooking temperature rise.

Cam saw the weariness forming deep lines in his face. She also thought he had lost weight. "How are you doing, Dad?"

"I'm doing fine. Your mama seems to be having more good days than usual lately. I'm glad for them, but you know what they say about the calm before the storm."

"Yeah, I know. I just hope she can make the best of them while she can. She seemed happy to be cooking jelly today."

"You know your mama, she loves the holidays."

"She certainly does. Is there anything else I can help you with?"

Ronny looked up at her with tears in his eyes. "You're doing so much already. I don't know what it would be that you're not already doing."

"If there's anything, please let me know."

"She has a doctor's appointment in Baton Rouge on the twenty-seventh. Will you go with us? Some of those medical terms I just don't understand."

"I'd be more than happy to go."

"Thanks. I'm going to walk over and use the restroom. Do you need anything?"

"Grab me a bottle of water if you would, please."

"Coming right up."

†

Ronny stepped outside of the cooking shed and looked up to see Wanda on her perch. An echo he didn't recognize was coming across the water. He lifted the radio to his mouth. "What's that noise, Wanda?"

Wanda chuckled. "It's Buster and his crew working on the love shack. Their hammer strikes are echoing across the water."

"Ah, that makes sense. You want something to drink?"

"I'll take a soda if Cam has one."

"Head on down and I'll bring it out to you."

Ronny went inside the cabin, pulled a chilled Coke from the refrigerator, and carried it out to the base of the tree. He handed it up to Wanda, who thanked him and scurried back up to her post. He returned inside to use the facilities. As he walked through Cam's bedroom, he smiled over at the bedside table, where a picture of her and Tab sat. He'd never seen it before, but the look they shared showed how much in love they were.

"I hope I haven't screwed that up for Cam," he grumbled to himself.

†

Cam reached for the bottle of water he offered and he sat next to her. "Tab only has two more days with us before she has to drive back to Monroe, right?"

"Yes, sir. Her mother's expecting her home Friday."

"Why don't the two of y'all spend the time together out here? Me and the girls can handle your mama and the house alone for a couple of days."

"We get enough time together, Dad."

"No, you don't, and I know Tab will be starting back to school again soon and you may not get a lot of time with her after that."

Cam knew her dad was correct. "You sure you wouldn't mind?"

"Absolutely not. You can do one thing for me, and that's fill the feeders. Just watch out for the Rougarou," he teased.

"Dear Lord, don't get me going on that again. That damned sow scared the bejesus out of me."

"After that enjoy your time together, maybe sleep in a couple of days."

"I wouldn't know how to sleep past six," Cam admitted. "My internal clock goes crazy around then."

"Maybe Tab will wear you out and you can learn what it's like to sleep in." He grinned.

His comment surprised Cam. It wasn't the first time he'd ever hinted he was aware of their relationship, but the sexual innuendo of his comment caught her off guard. "Maybe so." She grinned back at him.

"Are you up to leading a few hog hunts this year?"

"Yes. I think I know the property pretty well, but maybe Tab and I can do some research. She seems to like four wheeling."

"I've already got a few hunts lined up for late January and into February. Just daytime trips, no overnight deals. They are mostly just big-city middle-aged guys wanting the thrill of the hunt. Any hog they shoot will go in our freezers. They just want the heads for trophies."

"That's a real shame, but at least we'll eat well and get a good payday."

"Yes, we will." He looked over at the still. "Looks like the temperature is at cooking level. Would you mind going ahead and getting a fire started? We'll be getting a head soon and will need to check it with the fire."

"I'll be back shortly." Cam left the shed.

She laid and started a fire, then spent several minutes chopping more wood. It would be a long day of cooking, and if she and Tab were going to be spending some solo days at the camp, she wanted to make sure they had wood for campfires. When she returned to the shed, the first drops of 'shine were beginning to flow.

"You've got great timing. Have a seat and rest for a few, and when it's ready, I'll test the head."

Cam drained her bottle of water. "No argument there. I've chopped the rest of our wood. Maybe I'll drop a few more trees while Tab and I are out running around."

"Do I need to remind you that you're supposed to be relaxing with Tab? There will be time after she's gone, and you have younger sisters that would love to help."

Cam nodded in surrender. "That's true."

"Are we all set for Christmas?"

"I think so. The girls have finished their shopping; the meal's planned, so I can't think of anything else. Can you?"

"Sounds like you have all the bases covered."

"I hope so. If not, we'll make it work."

"I've been thinking about something lately that I wanted to run past you, if you're up for a serious conversation."

"Sure, Dad."

"Your mama's illness has got me thinking about our family's future. When things slow down this spring, I'd like us to officially register a family business and get incorporated. It would have some financial benefits for you girls moving forward."

Cam looked at him, frowning. "There isn't something else you're not telling me, is there? Everything's okay with you, right?"

"I'm fit as a fiddle. Your mama's health has just got me to thinking, and I want to know that after we're both gone, you girls will carry on the legacy of the St. Angelo family."

"So have you come up with a name of this corporation?"

"Funny you should ask. It just so happens, I have. Gator Girlz, Inc., using a *z* instead of *s* to be different. Gator tags are still our most profitable, legitimate business, so I thought it'd be fitting."

Cam smiled as the name sunk in. "I like it."

"I'd put you down as president and CEO with T and Karen as vice presidents. I think Wanda will make a good chief financial officer and she wants to study business when she graduates. I'd like to go ahead and start a college fund for her."

"What about Sandy?"

"She's so young. It's hard for me to determine what her future will be. T and Karen, I think will both be married off right after high school, but I think it will be you, Wanda, and Sandy who carry on the family businesses. Frankly, I don't see Sandy ever leaving the bayou, even to go to college. Her heart and soul rest here."

"I think you could be right."

"So that just leaves you to decide what your future is going to be. Will you return to school next fall or stay here to run the business?"

Cam opened her mouth to comment but Ronny stopped her. "There's no need for an answer now. I want you to weigh your options carefully before you make any decisions."

Cam sighed deeply as she sat back in her chair.

"I know it's a lot to spring on you all at once, given our current circumstance, but I want you to be prepared and not caught off guard like we've been with your mama."

"I understand, Dad; just don't get any wild notion of running off on us anytime soon."

"I plan on being here until the Good Lord calls me home. Right now, though, I'm going to test the head on that batch to see if we need to cook it down some. Care to join me?"

"Right behind ya."

"Careful, those eggs from breakfast have done a number on my system." He grinned.

"Thanks for the warning." She slapped him on the back and walked out of the shed in front of him to the fire pit.

"Let's see what we got here," he said and tossed the liquid into the fire. A pure blue flame ignited, bringing a smile to their faces. "That's what I wanted to see. Let's run this batch and put it in the cooling vat before starting another run. If we're lucky we might get twenty-five gallons cooked today."

"Are we using the five-gallon containers for your Baton Rouge customer?"

"Yep, he likes it that way. He can do his own bottling and save us the trouble. He probably doubles the price he pays us, but business is business."

"Ain't that the truth?" They walked back into the shed together. "Do you want to continue with the corn, or switch to the cane mash?"

"Let's finish up the corn, then do the cane. I think we'll have enough of the last watermelon for the season to run a small batch. It's such a nice festive color."

"We may want to plant more melons next year, the way the Red Bliss has become so popular," Cam said, talking about the watermelon 'shine.

"I'd like to try out some other flavors next year too. Maybe some apple and pear."

"It can't hurt to try. I bet the fruity blends will go over really well."

†

They cooked and chatted for several more hours before Wanda's voice crackled across the radio. "Lunch is on the way," she reported.

"Come on down outta dat tree and let's eat, then."

Cam had to chuckle at how her dad's Cajun would sneak out from time to time. She loved to hear it, especially when he was telling stories. It made the telling all that more hilarious.

They had just finished putting in the first batch of cane mash when T pulled up to the dock.

"Hey there," Cam said when Tab stepped off the boat. She took a picnic basket from her. "Good grief this is heavy."

"Your mama thought you might be hungry. She also sent four jars of jelly to you, before they disappeared."

"Did you enjoy making it?"

"Yes, it was very interesting. We're going to work on the grape jelly this afternoon. Your mama wanted to take a short break for a nap."

"She's not overdoing things, is she?" Ronny asked, concerned.

"No, sir, she's pretty much been directing traffic, and giving instructions, but we could tell she was tired."

"If she's not up to finishing this afternoon, we will convince her to do it another time," T told him.

"Good luck with that. You know your mama; once she starts a project, there's no quitting until it's done."

"That's true. So what did Mama send us for lunch?" Cam asked.

"There are turkey and ham sandwiches, and yes, before you ask, she put cranberry sauce on several turkey sandwiches for you, Cam," T said.

"I can't wait to sink my teeth into them," Cam replied.

"We've got a huge venison roast in the oven with vegetables, and several loaves of fresh bread rising. I just hope Sandy and Willow don't make so much racket, they drop."

Cam smiled. "Send both of them outside."

"Oh, trust me, they've been back and forth between the house and checking on Buster and his crew all morning."

"How's the love shack coming along?" Ronny asked.

"The flooring joists are in and they've managed about half the floor. Buster and Jeff are framing the sides, and I think they'll raise at least two walls before the time the sun goes down."

"Coming right along. The trusses will be delivered tomorrow, right?"

"Yes, sir, that's why they're trying to get the walls framed out today."

"She keeps going to the living room to peek out the window at it," Tab joked.

Cam set the basket on the kitchen table and started spreading out sandwiches. "Pour us some tea, please, Wanda."

"Did y'all eat already?" Ronny asked.

Tab nodded. "Yes, sir, but I admit those turkey sandwiches look good."

"Try one," Cam encouraged.

"Maybe just a half." Tab smiled as she cut a sandwich in half.

After lunch they filled three of the five-gallon containers with the cooled 'shine. The last of the cane was cooking, and then they would cook the last batch of the season of Red Bliss.

"Would you mind if I keep a quart of the Red Bliss out here?" Cam asked.

"You don't even have to ask. Take what you want."

"We'll see how far we can make it stretch," Cam replied.

†

"Let's go, Willow," Cam said after she and Wanda had finished loading the feed onto the boat. "See y'all soon," she called out to the family as Tab stepped onto the boat, and Willow jumped in beside her.

"So I get you all to myself for the next two days?"

Cam smiled. "I'm all yours. We have one chore to do, and then the rest of the time is all ours to do what we want."

Tab stroked Willow as they drove across the bayou. She was excited and surprised by this turn of events, but a small part of her felt guilty for taking Cam away from her family and caring for her mama. When they pulled up to the dock, she turned to Cam. "Are you sure? Your family needs you."

"They will be fine for two days. I need you."

Tab couldn't argue with Cam. They did need some time together. She would return to school when break was over, and then the season would start. Their time together would be severely limited then. She was most surprised to find that going out to the cabin was Ronny's idea. That was the best validation of their relationship Tab could ever hope to receive. It felt amazing to know that he realized how much they loved one another.

She stepped off the boat and tied the mooring line. "Do you want me to bring the Gator around so we can load it?"

"That would be great," Cam smiled.

Willow rushed ahead of Tab as she walked to the camp for the keys. She reached inside the cabin to grab them and walked to the shed.

"Let's go, girl," she called and Willow jumped onto the seat beside her. Tab drove the Gator to the dock and helped Cam load the bags of feed. "All we need is the buckets to mix the feed, right?"

"You're turning into a mighty fine country girl," Cam said as she stepped forward and kissed Tab.

"I have a great teacher."

"So, my love. What would you like to do tonight?"

"I'd love to be naked with you and wallow in that big old comfy bed with you until we're breathless."

"Well, hot damn, let me put the Gator away. Be right back." Tab and Willow walked to the porch to wait for her return.

Cam was grinning as she parked the Gator and walked back to the cabin, where she took Tab's hand and led her inside. She checked Willow's food and water and placed several treats and her favorite chew toy, one of Cam's old work boots, on the dog's bed.

"Now, I'm all yours."

Tab lit several candles in the room and began to slowly undress. Cam kicked off her boots and pulled her shirt over her head.

There was no need for silence as they spent the night loving one another. Tab got her wish, and Cam collapsed beside her breathless from their lovemaking. She pulled Tab into her arms and soon after, the rumble of thunder filled the air.

"It sounds like we've loved up a storm. I better take Willow outside before the rain arrives." Cam climbed from the bed and slipped on a T-shirt and shorts. "Let's go, Willow," she called.

She opened the door and Willow rushed out ahead of her. Cam sat on the steps as she made a circuit of the yard until she found the right spot. She was trotting back to Cam when another sound broke the night. The bellow of a large gator filled the air, and Willow froze in her tracks as her hackles rose and her eyes searched the dark banks.

"Don't worry, girl, he's a long way off."

Willow trotted back to her and sat between her legs. As Cam stroked her hair, she could smell the rain in the air and see the distant flash of lightning. The rumbling of thunder concealed the opening of the door as Tab stepped outside to sit down beside her.

"I understand why you love this place so much," Tab said, looking into her eyes.

"Its home, and always will be. No matter where my heart takes me, my soul will always rest here."

Tab placed an arm around Cam's waist and laid her head on her shoulder as they listened to the night on the bayou. When the raindrops started to fall, Willow bolted for the door.

"Are you afraid you'll melt?" Tab called after her.

Cam smiled and followed them inside, then locked the door behind her. By the time she reached the bedroom, Tab was again naked in the bed, and Willow stretched out on the foot of the bed. She slipped out of her clothes and climbed in beside Tab as the rain began pelting the tin roof. Tab turned to snuggle into Cam, and Willow crept up the bed to rest beside Cam's hip. Wrapped in a cocoon of love, Cam let their warmth and the sound of the rain deliver her to sleep.

CHAPTER EIGHT

They spent the next two days exploring the Island. After filling the feeders, Cam drove them deeper into the bayou and they circled the boundary of the St. Angelo's property. Cam kept a sharp eye out for signs of deer and wild hogs. The feral-hog-population explosion had made its way from Texas to Louisiana, and she knew that in addition to the hunts they would hold after the first of the year, she and her dad would hunt to cull some of the population. If they were left to run rampant, the hogs' voracious feeding and breeding could destroy the environments of the other wildlife in the area. What meat they couldn't store, they would give to families in town. The bayou and its people took care of one another.

Cam enjoyed cooking for Tab and started out their days with breakfast in bed. As she feared, there was no sleeping in for her, but waking up early gave her time to care for Willow and watch Tab as she slept until Cam delivered a tray of breakfast. They would make love, then shower before leaving to explore the Island. Cam packed leftover biscuits and meat for an easy lunch.

The night before Tab was due to leave, Cam pulled out a bottle of chilled Red Bliss and poured them a small glass.

"This is very tasty," Tab remarked after taking a sip.

"Be careful, it'll sneak up on you."

Cam had grilled steak dinners for their last night together. When they finished eating, she walked into the bedroom and returned with several small packages. She sat down beside Tab and handed her the presents. "Merry Christmas."

"I'm sorry; I didn't bring anything besides Willow."

"You gave me the best present I could ask for: a faithful companion, who will comfort me when you're not here. She's perfect, not just for me but the rest of the family. I think Sandy has a new best friend."

Tab opened the largest package to find a box with a pair of new work boots.

"I think it is time you had a pair of your own. You can leave them here for your next visit if you'd like."

The next box held a beautiful tooled-leather bracelet Cam had worked on for days. Tab took it from the box and snapped it around her wrist. "It's beautiful."

Tab's heart raced as she picked up the final, smaller box and unwrapped it. Inside was a gold rope chain with a solid gold heart. She looked up at Cam with tears in her eyes.

"No matter where you go, Baton Rouge or Durham, my heart will always be with you. Thank you for making me whole."

Tab's hands were shaking and she fumbled trying to get the necklace secured around her neck. Cam smiled, took it from her, and fastened it for her. "There," she said and kissed Tab.

"Thanks for the beautiful gifts," Tab said as she wrapped her arms around Cam.

The sounds of their loving echoed through the bedroom as they loved the night away, unsure of when they'd have another chance to be together.

†

The next morning Cam helped her pack her bags to load into the boat. They'd share a last breakfast with the family before Tab would drive back to Monroe. When they loaded the last bag, Cam kissed her deeply.

"One for the road," she said as tears filled Tab's eyes. "Please don't cry." She pulled her into her arms.

When Tab stepped away, she looked at Cam. "I'll be strong for you, and your family."

Cam nodded and stepped into the boat. "Will you cast us off?"

Tab untied the line and joined her, then took a seat beside Cam.

The girls had cooked a monstrous breakfast to see Tab off. Everyone ate their fill, and Tab hugged everyone while wishing them a Merry Christmas. When she hugged Camille, she held on a little longer.

"I love you, Mama," Cam heard her whisper.

Tab patted Willow's head and took Cam's hand to walk out to her loaded car. "I'll call you tonight. Love you."

"Love you more," Cam replied, and opened the door for her. "Be safe and I'll be waiting on your call."

Cam watched her leave, waving until Tab's car was no longer in sight, then walked back inside to her family. "That was one great breakfast."

"I'm glad y'all enjoyed it. The girls did it all on their own." Camille wrapped Cam in her arms as Cam trembled. "She'll be back," she whispered.

Cam nodded as she stepped back from her mama. "You know, I've been thinking."

"Here we go again," Wanda joked.

"What's on your mind, Cam?" Ronny asked.

"I was thinking it was time you and I thin out some wild hogs. They are plentiful on the Island. If we can find us a big boy, it's time for a pig pickin'. I was thinking for New Year's?"

"I know several families in town that would appreciate some fresh hogs," he said. "Let's do it."

Wanda wiggled in her seat. "Can I go this year?"

Ronny looked at Cam, who nodded. "I think she's ready."

"If you'll bring in two, I'll get Buster and Jeff to dig out the pit and help cook them," T said.

Karen's eyes lit up at the mention of Jeff, Buster's younger brother, and Cam knew she had taken a shine to him. "That sounds like a good plan. Trust me, there's plenty hogs to choose from."

"I bet we could even talk Tony into processing them for us, if there was an extra boar in there for him," Ronny said.

"I'll leave that up to you to arrange." Cam glanced at her mama, who was grinning from ear to ear. "Do you have any plans for us today?"

"Nothing I can't handle. Why?"

"I'd thought I'd take these two"—she pointed to Wanda and Sandy—"and cut down that old oak the lightning hit last week. If we're gonna be having a pig pickin' we need lots of wood."

Ronny looked at Cam. "There's an old apple tree at the Rickards' place that needs to be taken down. I bet we could barter a small hog for the applewood."

"You work on getting the applewood and we'll start on the old oak," Cam said.

"I'll make a call this morning." Ronny smiled.

"We'll take the tractor and small trailer if you don't need it."

"Nope, if the Rickards are good, I'll take T and we'll go ahead and take the smaller apple tree down, cut it to lengths, and after Christmas we can go pick it up," Ronny said.

Cam looked at Karen. "You okay helping Mama with lunch and getting some dinner started?"

Karen smiled. "Absolutely. I think I'll try my hand on chicken and dumplings again."

"We can get the ham, Turducken, and the rest of the dishes ready for tomorrow too," Camille said. "They'll need to go in the oven early in the morning."

"I don't think early will be a problem with Squirt in the house," Cam teased.

"I can remember when you were the leader of the pack, waking up early and racing to the tree," Camille reminded her. "It wasn't that long ago."

"Ha! You're so right, Mama." She kissed her and turned to her sisters. "Let's go, daylight's a-wasting."

†

With Wanda's help, Cam hitched the trailer to the tractor, and her two younger sisters climbed onto it as she grabbed a chainsaw, gas mix, and bar oil, then placed them in the back with her sisters.

"Cam, do you think there's any way we can talk Dad into letting me go on the hunt with y'all?" Sandy asked with pleading eyes.

"I don't know, Squirt. Hog hunting can be dangerous. Those boars are quick, and those tusks are sharp. I'm sorry, but it may be too distracting for you to join the hunt, because we'd have to worry about your safety. We could probably talk him into letting you stay with the Gator and bringing it to us when we've made a kill."

"Well, at least that would be something."

"Actually, that would be a big help to us." Cam climbed onto the tractor. "It would save us a bunch of walking."

Sandy beamed at the prospect.

"I'll talk to Dad about it tonight."

"Thanks, Cam."

Cam smiled at her baby sister and put the tractor in gear. "Hang on, this first part's gonna be bumpy."

†

Several hours later, Ronny walked out to where they were cutting, carrying the picnic basket. "Time for a lunch break," he called out when Cam stopped the saw.

"That sounds good to me," she replied, and walked over to the trailer.

"Y'all have done well this morning," he said, surveying the stacked wood on the trailer. "Would you mind some more help?"

"We'll never refuse help." Cam looked at him curiously. "What did you find out about the applewood?"

"The tree is down, and with Buddy Rickards' help, cut into small sections. I told him we'd be by after Christmas to haul it back here. He was very excited about getting some wild hog."

"Ya know, Dad, I was thinking"—she winked at Sandy—"Squirt here could go on the hunt with us but stay with the Gator until we had a kill. Then we could radio our location to her and she could bring the Gator to us."

"Not a bad idea." Ronny grinned. "Are you up for that, Squirt?"

"Heck yes," Sandy nearly screamed.

"Y'all work on these sandwiches while I go get my saw. Are you doing okay on gas mix?"

"Yes, sir, but if we have more bar oil, will you bring it?"

"I just opened a fresh bottle this morning. I'll be back in a bit."

Sandy waited until her dad was out of hearing range before she said, "Thanks, Cam."

"Oh, don't be thanking me just yet. We've still got a lot of work to do. Some of this wood needs splitting before we can use it. I'll do that while you and Wanda carry and stack the rest."

"Do you think we'll finish it today?" Wanda asked.

"Probably not, but at least we can get a good start on it. Eat up so we can get back at it."

Ronny returned as they were finishing lunch. "So, boss lady, what do you want me to do?"

Cam chuckled. "I can work on the bigger limbs with the larger saw if you don't mind cutting those into lengths the girls can carry," she said, nodding to a pile of limbs she had already trimmed.

"Not a problem," he answered and started the saw.

Cam took a long drink of water, then checked the levels on her saw and topped off the gas and bar-oil levels.

She watched Sandy and Wanda carrying the logs Ronny had already cut. *I don't think any of us will have trouble sleeping tonight. Not even me.* She walked over to the fallen tree and continued cutting on the larger branches.

Darkness was falling as they finished loading the trailer with the sections they had cut.

"Any more and I don't think that old tractor will pull it," Ronny said as he placed his saw on a limb. "This will give us a heck of a good pile for cooking."

"Why don't you drive the tractor, and the girls and I will carry the saws and supplies. You know how the old girl handles better than I do. We'll drop these off and meet you out by the fire pit," Cam said.

"That's a deal too good to pass up." Ronny grinned.

Cam and her sisters picked up the picnic basket and supplies and started for home. When they arrived, they dropped the saws in the shed and walked around to the fire pit. As they rounded the corner, they were surprised to find Buster, Jeff, and two other men digging out a new pit.

"I'm glad you guys are doing that job," she told Buster.

"We ran out of daylight for working on the house, so I thought we'd go ahead and knock this new pit out, especially with three extra shovels." He introduced two of his friends from town.

"We appreciate your help," she told the men.

One of them looked up at her. "Buster says you're one heck of a hunter and you'll be killing off a bunch of wild hogs. Do you reckon we could talk you out of a couple? Your idea for a pig pickin's got our mouths watering too."

"I think that would be well worth the price of digging this pit," she agreed. "This is huge, probably big enough to hold three or four hogs."

"Well you know, Cam, I got to thinking after T told me about your idea. Dad's got a piece of fence paneling he's not using that will make an excellent top for this pit, so we dug it for size. I'll plant a few four-by-four posts to secure the corners and we can cook like crazy."

"That's a great idea, Buster. We're working on the wood. Dad's got us some applewood coming later in the week."

"You leave the rest of this up to us. You provide the hogs and we'll do the rest. As soon as your dad gets here, we'll get that wood stacked for you too. Got some that needs splitting?"

"Yes, but not a whole lot."

"I can do that after Christmas," Jeff piped in. "I'll come early before we start back on the house."

When Ronny arrived with the trailer full of wood, Cam brought him up to speed on the plans, then joined the others unloading and stacking the wood. Within the hour, a nice pile was ready for the cookout.

"I do love it when a plan comes together," Ronny said as he wiped his forehead.

"Merry Christmas, everyone," Buster said, and he and the men left for home after he got a kiss from T.

Camille walked to the door and stuck her head out. "You all look tired and hungry. "Come wash up and have some supper."

†

Cam was exhausted. After she finished eating she and Willow drove back to the Island, she looked at her phone to see she had missed two calls from Tab in all the activity of the day. She moored the boat, grabbed a cold beer, and watched Willow play in the yard while she sat on the steps to call Tab.

"Hey, sweetie. I'm sorry I missed your calls." She told Tab what they had been doing all day and their plans for a gigantic pig pickin'. "You know, if you decide to go back to campus early, you, Ruth, and Liz could join us for New Year's. There will be plenty of food, and they can join us out here." She smiled at Tab's answer. "Call them soon so they don't make plans, okay? I love you too. Merry Christmas. Call me when you can tomorrow."

Cam sat on the steps until she finished her beer, then called Willow. "It's time to go inside, little girl. Mama is in desperate need of a shower."

Cam stripped out of her dirty clothes and tossed them in the hamper. Her gaze went to her closet, and she smiled when she saw the brand-new pair of work boots she had given Tab, sitting next to the old pair Tab usually wore. Seeing a part of Tab still present in the silent cabin warmed her heart. She walked to the bathroom, showered, and

151

collapsed onto the bed. She barely remembered setting her alarm. She probably wouldn't need it, but she wanted to be up early enough to arrive home to make fresh biscuits and gravy for Christmas breakfast. Her mama had made that a tradition for almost twenty years, and now it was her turn to keep it going.

†

Christmas Morning dawned cooler than it had in years. Cam woke, dressed, and traveled across the water through a low ground fog. She could find home through the dark of night, so a bit of fog wouldn't keep her away. She slowed when she drew close, and pulled up next to the dock with perfection, then tied off and looked up at the house. A light was on in the kitchen.

"Someone beat us already," she told Willow.

Cam smiled when she crept through the back door to find her mama getting ready to start breakfast.

"Merry Christmas, Mama," Cam said as she hugged her from behind, then kissed her cheek.

"Merry Christmas, Cam. I was just getting ready to start breakfast."

"Not this year. I've got this, but you can pour us some coffee and keep me company."

Camille looked at Cam with tears glistening in her eyes. "I'll pour us some coffee, but I need to help with breakfast."

"Your biscuits are so much better than mine. You feel like whipping us up a batch, and I'll do the sausage and gravy?"

Camille smiled. "Turn the oven to Preheat for me." She pulled down two coffee mugs and poured them full.

Cam went to the refrigerator and pulled out the sausages she would cook. Camille was looking at her when she turned back around. "What, Mama?"

"I'm going to miss this so much. Cooking with you and the girls," she said, then turned away.

Cam placed the sausages on the counter, walked over to her, and took Camille in her arms. "You will always be with us, Mama."

Cam looked over Camille's head to see that her dad had walked in and lifted a hand to ask him to give them a minute. He nodded and stood still.

"I'm sorry, Cam." She stepped back and wiped her eyes.

"Don't worry, Mama; we'll do our best to get along. I promise I'll do everything I can to make you proud."

"You always have. I couldn't be prouder of any child of mine."

Ronny's tears were flowing down his cheeks as he entered the kitchen and hugged his wife. "I couldn't agree more."

"I have two wonderful parents who have taught me everything I know." Cam wiped back her tears as she smiled at them.

"Is there anything I can do?" he asked.

"Grab a cup of coffee, sit at the counter, and keep us company. This kitchen is already crowded," Camille said and bumped her hip into Cam.

Cam smiled at her parents, then opened a cabinet to pull out a frying pan and a cookie sheet for biscuits. She cherished every moment as she and her mama cooked their final Christmas breakfast together.

When the smell of cooking sausage filled the air, the others started to wake, and they came to the kitchen one after another, with Christmas wishes for all.

"Good morning and Merry Christmas, my babies," Camille said. "Breakfast or presents first?"

Normally they would opt for presents, but the girls seemed to sense the importance of this breakfast. "Breakfast first, Mama," Karen answered.

"Have a seat, then. It will be ready in a bit. Karen, you can come get dishes, and your sisters can help you set the table."

"Yes, Mama," Karen said and joined them in the kitchen.

When Camille pulled out the pan of biscuits, Cam moved the rack lower in the oven and slid the ham and Turducken into cook before joining them at the table.

It was a simple meal but would be hearty enough to hold them until midafternoon when they would have a huge meal. Cam took her seat next to her dad and was about to take a bite when her mama called out.

"Cameron St, Angelo, you've finally outdone my gravy." She smiled.

"Thanks, Mama, I'm glad you approve. I had a great teacher."

"This is a great meal," Ronny agreed. "Eat up, everyone."

†

They all quickly cleared the kitchen and took a seat in the living room. Presents filled the floor around the Christmas tree.

"Dad, will you play Santa this year?" Camille asked as she eased down in her recliner.

"I'd love to, Mama," he said and walked to the tree to pick up the first gift.

The family opened present after present and cherished each of the gifts they were given. When the last box was alone under the tree, Camille cleared her throat.

"The last box has your dad's name on it, but it's for all of you. Please open it, my love."

Ronny picked up the box and carried it to the couch. He began to carefully open it, with all eyes fixed on him. He opened the lid and pulled out a beautiful hand-carved nativity scene. His eyes shined with tears as he looked at his wife.

"I know we've talked about it for years," Camille said to him. "I wanted to leave you all something special to remember this last Christmas together. I won't be here in body, but I'll be with you every day," she promised.

"It's beautiful, Mama," Cam said.

"Clear off the coffee table for me, girls," Ronny said, then gently placed the nativity scene in the middle. "It's perfect." He walked over and kissed Camille, who looked at him with pain in her eyes.

The emotion of the morning had clearly taken a toll on her mama. "Why don't you lie down for a bit, Mama?" Cam asked.

"I think I will. You've got a good start on the meal, but don't let me sleep the day away," she told Ronny.

"We won't, my love."

Willow left the chew bone Santa had brought her and followed Camille and Ronny to the bedroom. Cam knew it was pointless to call her back, so she let her go, knowing that Willow would climb up in the bed when her mama was settled and snuggle into her to give her comfort. She passed the room later and saw her mama's hand resting on Willow's back as the pup's head stretched across her stomach. She took out her phone and snapped a quick photo to send to Tab. Her mother's smile as she slept was priceless. Cam leaned against the doorframe for several minutes watching them, until her dad came looking for her.

"She looks peaceful, doesn't she?"

"Yes, Dad, she does."

"Wanda is asking for you. She wants you to take her over to the Island so she can sight in the new rifle we got her."

"You got everything under control here?"

"Yeah, I think I can handle things for a bit." He smiled.

"Just don't let the turducken scorch, or Mama will shoot both of us."

"I promise I'll keep an eye on it. Take Squirt with you, please. She's starting to pace."

"We won't be long, I promise." Cam kissed his cheek and went in search of her sisters.

†

Cam attended her mama's appointment, and the news wasn't positive. Without treatment, the cancer had spread farther into her organs and bones, accounting for her increasing pain. The doctor held her mama's hand as he spoke to her, and Cam appreciated his gentle kindness.

"I'm going to up the strength of your pain medications. Have you been taking them regularly?"

Camille looked up at Cam and her husband. "I've been waiting until the pain is too much to bear. I don't want to sleep through the rest of what time I have left."

"I can understand that but waiting that long dulls the effect of the medications. Don't delay between doses. That will help you manage the pain better. I can add a second medication and keep the dosage the same as what you are currently taking." He offered her a smile.

"Whatever you feel is best."

"The label will read every four hours, but if three or more hours have passed, then feel free to take the next dose. I want to prevent as much of the pain as we can."

"Yes, thanks, Doctor." Ronny looked at Camille. "Do you need to use the restroom before we get back on the road?"

"Yes."

"I'll take her." Cam stood and helped her mama into a restroom down the hall.

†

Ronny waited until they had left the room before turning to the doctor. "Her time is getting close, isn't it?"

The doctor's smile faded. "I'm afraid so, Mr. St. Angelo. A few weeks at best. Are you and the family still able to care for her at home?"

"We make do. It's hard for everyone, but Camille wants to stay there as long as possible."

"I can understand that. I'll arrange for a Hospice nurse to begin visits and order an injection if these medications are not working well for her. I assume she has her affairs in order."

157

A tear slid down Ronny's cheek. "As much as they can be, I reckon." He offered his hand to the doctor, who took it and pulled him into an embrace.

"Call me anytime you have questions. I pray the end will be as painless as possible."

Ronny nodded. "Thank you, Doc." He stepped through the door to wait on his wife and daughter and brushed back his tears.

†

The hunt went great with three of them shooting, and they were able to cull twelve boars and young hogs over two days. They delivered them to LB's for processing, and then distributed across town. Cam and Wanda picked out two that were the perfect size for the pig pickin', and picked them up on the thirty-first. Buster and the boys would put them on to cook that night and tend to them until they cooked to perfection. They were just arriving home when Tab, Ruth, and Liz pulled into the yard.

"That's great timing. We could use some muscle," she called out to them.

Ruth stepped out of the passenger side and flexed. "You called?"

Cam pulled her into a hug. "I'm glad y'all could make it."

"Me too. I was afraid we'd blow up on the way," Liz said as she uncurled her long legs from the backseat.

"Blow up?" Cam asked.

"We brought something for the occasion," Tab said as she popped the trunk. Cam peeked inside to discover it filled with an assortment of fireworks.

"Oh, heck yeah. Great idea, sweetie."

Wanda peeked and saw what made her grin. "This is gonna be fun."

"Why don't you take those to the shed, and we'll carry these coolers out to the pit." Cam walked around to open Tab's door and pulled Tab tight against her. "I've missed you."

"I've missed you more." Tab grinned.

"Doubtful, but I'll let you win for now." She let go of Tab to hug Liz. "I've missed y'all too."

"How's everything going?" Liz asked.

Cam shrugged. "As well as can be expected, I reckon. Mama has her good days, and bad. We had a great Christmas, but I can see her going downhill. The doctor's report wasn't good."

Liz hugged her again. "Just remember we love you, and your family."

"Other than lugging these coolers around back, what else can we do to help?" Ruth asked.

"We can check on what the girls are rounding up for supper and see if they need help. Other than that, I think we're set until tomorrow. The boys will cook all night, so Buster is bringing a keg; I thought we'd help him tap. We can do the fireworks tonight too."

They carried two coolers under the shelter of the pavilion. The coolers were packed with dry ice, to keep the hog meat cold, and the hogs would remain there until they went into the pit. Ronny and Sandy had arranged some of the oakwood they had cut in the pit. All it needed was lighting. Buster and the boys would be out later to season the meat and get the coals started, and then the fun would begin.

"Let's head inside," Cam suggested.

Camille looked up as they entered the kitchen, and her smile lit the room. "I'm so glad y'all could make it."

"We wouldn't miss it for anything, Mama," Tab said and hugged her gently.

Ruth stepped up to hug her and kissed her cheek. "What you got cooking that smells so good?"

"A little bit of this, a little bit of that." Camille grinned. "Hey, Liz." Camille hugged her. "Have y'all had lunch?"

"Yes, ma'am, we stopped along the way."

"Well, I certainly hope y'all have brought good appetites. It's feasting time around here. Cam, will you set up the fry cookers and then take the girls over to the Island to get settled?"

"Sure, Mama. What are we gonna be cooking?"

"The girls have spent the last two hours making boudin wraps to cook, and we've got fresh cracklins to go with them."

"Have they already been cooked down for frying?" Cam asked.

"Cooked, scored, and seasoned, just waiting for you to deep fry them," Camille answered.

"What else?"

"Catfish filets, and of course your hush puppies, if you don't mind cooking all that."

"I've got plenty help to recruit. Ruth's pretty handy around a fryer, and we've got two excellent gophers to run for what we need."

"Good, your sisters and I will take care of the inside foods. We've already got a huge bowl of slaw made. We can whip up some garlic grits when it's closer to time, and we've got two cakes in the oven."

"I reckon I'd better get a move on, then. Tab, can you and Liz grab your bags while Ruth and I set up the fryers? Do we have oil, Mama?"

"T took two brand-new jugs out earlier. They are in the shed with the cookers."

"Oh, ladies, do you want to tell the girls what you brought for tonight?" Cam prompted.

Tab smiled at Sandy. "We've got fireworks to let off later."

Camille's eyes smiled. "That will be so much fun."

"All right!" Sandy rushed around and hugged each of them. "I can't wait."

Cam looked at Sandy. "Have you got the catfish soaking in buttermilk?"

"Way ahead of ya. They've been soaking for hours." Sandy chuckled.

"Now why doesn't that surprise me?"

"Can I help you cook tonight?" Sandy pleaded.

"I was counting on you to help," Cam said and Sandy smiled proudly. Cam looked at her watch. "If we're back at four to cook, will that be good, Mama?"

"That should be perfect," Camille answered. "Buster and Jeff should be here around then with an ice-cold keg."

"That sounds good. See you then." Cam kissed her mama and turned to the others. "Let's get to work, ladies."

Liz and Tab went back through the front of the house to get their bags, with Sandy and Willow hot on their heels. Cam and Ruth walked out to the shed to pull out the fryers and propane tanks. Wanda followed, carrying the jugs of oil.

When they had everything set, Cam turned to her sisters. "We'll see you at four. You want to keep Willow to play with?"

"Heck yeah," Sandy said, and they took off running across the yard.

"Let's go get you settled at the camp." Cam smiled and led her friends to the boat.

†

"No wonder you talk about this place all the time," Ruth said to Tab. "This is a nice little hideout. Close enough to family to get to them fast, but still have a place of your own."

"It is perfect for us." Tab smiled, then turned to Cam and pulled her in for a kiss. "It's our home."

"The second bedroom isn't big, but it'll do for this trip," Cam said. "I'm not sure how much sleeping we're going to be doing."

"Make yourselves at home, and we can crash in the living room for a bit and have a beer." Cam picked up Tab's bag. "I'm so glad you're here."

"Me too, baby." Tab kissed her. "You look tired. Have you been sleeping okay?"

"Willow is a great bed buddy, but she's not you. I've missed snuggling into you."

"You've got me for three more nights before we have to head back. Coach asked about you and said to tell you hello."

"Send her my regards. How's the team looking?"

"Good, but we miss you in the lineup, and field. Parker's been working out at shortstop, but she's no Cam St. Angelo."

"Sandy's already asking if we can catch a game." Cam forced a smile.

"Do you have a copy of the schedule? I don't have a new roomie, so you can stay at the apartment when you come to town," Tab said.

"Yes, thanks. Let's go visit with the gals." Cam took her hand and led her to the fridge to pull out beers.

Liz and Ruth walked into the kitchen and took an icy-cold beer each. Cam smiled at her friends. "How's school going for y'all?"

"Grad school has been a breeze so far." Ruth chuckled and took a sip.

Liz smiled. "I've been lucky too. I only have three classes left until I graduate."

"I wish I could say the same. I've got some butt-kicking classes this semester. Traveling for ball will make them even harder," Tab groaned.

"Buckle down, girlie, you've only got one more year before law school." Cam smiled.

"Damn, you sound like my dad," Tab teased.

"You're looking good. Have you grown taller?" Ruth asked.

"I have with all this hard work. I've grown an inch. I had to buy longer jeans." Cam chuckled. "It's been good, though, being here for Mama and the family."

"She looks pretty good. I didn't see your dad. How's he doing?" Ruth asked.

"He's stressed as you would imagine, but good. He's making a last-minute delivery to a customer in Texas. He should be back this afternoon."

"Sandy looks like she's shot up a couple of inches since ball camp too," Liz said.

"Growing like a weed but staying slim. Strong as a baby ox, though."

"The love shack's coming along pretty good," Tab said.

"Love shack?" Liz smirked.

"That's the name for the house Buster is building for T. It should be done well ahead of the wedding this June," Cam shared.

"That will be exciting," Liz said.

Cam frowned. "She and Mama have been working hard to plan it down to the decorations on the cake."

"I'm sorry, Cam, we didn't mean to make you feel sad."

"It's not your fault, Liz. It is what it is."

"I know today and tomorrow will be pretty full, but do you think we can get some four-wheeling in?" Tab asked.

Cam's smile returned. "Yeah, that sounds like fun."

"Tab had us rolling on the floor with laughter telling us about her snipe-hunt adventure and the Rougarou." Ruth chuckled.

"She's a real country girl now that she's been muddin' and snipe hunting. One heck of a fisherwoman too," Cam bragged.

"I can't wait to see Tab Fortner covered in mud." Liz laughed.

"Trust me, it's a beautiful sight." Cam leaned over and kissed her. "You want a sweatshirt or jacket for tonight? It's going to get cooler."

"I'll get it. I want to change into my boots too." Tab smiled and leaned down to kiss her in return before disappearing to the bedroom.

Cam looked at her friends. "How's she doing?"

"Missing you like crazy, even worse than we are." Ruth chuckled. "She actually made a comment the other day about skipping out on law school to come live with you."

"What? She can't do that!"

"Yeah, she could, Cam," Liz said.

"No, no, no," Cam said. "She can't give up her dream like that."

"Relax, my friend, it's not happening yet," Ruth soothed.

Tab walked back into the room wearing her new boots, carrying one of Cam's sweatshirts. She glanced from one woman to the other, as if she could feel the tension in the room. "Are we ready to go?"

She looked at Liz, who smiled back at her. "Let me grab a coat."

"Everything okay?" she asked Cam.

"Yes, sweetie, it's fine. How do those boots feel?"

"They're like slipping my feet into soft velvet. They fit perfect."

"That's great. They look good on you."

"All set," Liz said as she walked back in the room.

†

By the time they returned to the homestead, Buster and Jeff had arrived and tapped the keg. They lit the fire in the pit and worked on seasoning the hogs while waiting for the coals to burn down. Ruth and Cam had a plan for the cooking. Ruth would cook the boudin wraps while Cam worked on the cracklins. The crowd could munch on those until the fish and hush puppies were done.

Cam walked into the kitchen to get the tray of food to cook and smiled when she found Wanda and Karen mixing her hush-puppy mix for her.

"Good job, ladies. Cover it and place it in the fridge until it's time."

"You got it," Karen answered.

"Can you rustle us up a paper sack and pour some of the cracklin season in it for me, Wanda?"

"No problem."

"As I take the cracklins out of the grease and cut them, you can drop them in the bag and give it a good shake, then spread them out on a tray to go with the boudin. Pepper Jack?" she asked.

"Yep, Mama's favorite," T answered.

"Pull us out a couple of cookie sheets, and line them with paper towels so the wraps and cracklins can drain."

"I've got that covered," Wanda said. "I'll bring them out with the seasoning."

"I reckon I'd better get to cooking. Where's Mama?"

"Taking a nap," Karen said. "She wants to stay up until midnight and thought she'd need a nap for that."

"Okay, then, here I go." Cam picked up two trays filled with the wraps and cracklins and carried them outside. Ruth had already gotten the cookers started heating the oil.

"Oh, my goodness. My mouth is watering already. I haven't had boudin and fresh-cooked cracklins in forever," Ruth said as she sat the trays of food down.

"I hope you like Pepper-Jack cheese. These are fully loaded."

"Perfect." Ruth grinned.

Ronny walked outside to greet his guests. "Welcome back, ladies. I hope you don't mind being put to work."

"No, sir, we're glad to help out any way we can," Ruth said and hugged him.

Tab carried over two glasses of draft beer for the cooks. "Can I get you a glass?"

Ronny smiled. "That would be great. Then I'll go check on the boys. I've gotten several calls from folks thanking us for the hog meat," he told Cam.

Cam smiled back at him. "It was a win-win situation all around. We culled the feral population, and folks are eating well." She picked up a knife, cut the slab of meat into manageable sections for cooking, and slipped it into the hot grease.

Ruth filled her cooker with the boudin wraps and picked up her beer. "To a great night," she said and tipped glasses with her friends.

Cam took a sip of her beer and saw Sandy and Willow bolt from the house. "I swear she doesn't have a slow gear anymore," she told her friends as Sandy rushed up to her.

"You snuck in on me. Wait 'til you see what Willow has learned today."

"Show us," Cam said.

"Willow, sit." Willow sat back on her haunches. "Wait for it." Sandy placed a small dog treat on the bridge of the pup's nose. "Wait." Sandy looked at Cam, then back at Willow. "Okay, now," she instructed.

They watched in amazement as Willow tossed the treat in the air, then captured it with her mouth. The group clapped for them. "Great job, Sandy. How long did that take for her to learn?" Cam asked.

"Only a few tries." She turned to Tab. "You picked us out a smart one."

"I think you're a pretty good trainer too," Tab said.

"Are you still helping me with hush puppies later?" Cam asked.

"You bet I am."

"Will you run inside and ask Wanda to bring her paper sack out? This first batch is almost done."

They watched Sandy fly across the yard. "See what I mean?" Cam chuckled as she carefully took the first slab out of the hot grease.

"Let me cut those cubes while you start on the next batch," Liz said as she picked up a sturdy fork and the knife.

"Thanks, but be careful. They're hot still, and the grease may pop at you," Cam warned.

"I'll have some wraps done in just a minute too," Ruth said as the eggroll-like goodies were turning a nice crisp golden-brown.

Working together, Liz and Wanda prepared the first batch of cracklins and dropped them onto the cookie sheet next to the wraps Ruth had taken out of the grease.

"Now comes the hard part," Cam teased. "Waiting for them to cool enough to eat."

Cam looked up when the back door opened, and her mama moved cautiously down the steps. "I thought I smelled cracklins."

"Tab, will you grab Mama a chair, please?"

"Sure thing. Mama, what would you like a drink?" she asked as Camille settled into a chair.

"Like? I'd like one of those Abita', but I'd better stick to a soda."

"I'll get it for you. A Coke or Sprite?" Sandy asked.

"A Sprite, please, baby. Get one of your sisters to give you some of those small paper plates too," Camille requested. "Those hush puppies look delicious."

"They should be cool enough in just a few more minutes, Mama," Cam assured her.

Liz and Tab pulled their chairs next to Camille's as they waited for the food to cool. Sandy returned with a bottled soda for her mama and placed a stack of small plates on the table.

Camille smiled at her baby girl. "What are your sisters doing?"

"Frosting the cakes. They said they'd be out in a minute now that the food's cooking," Sandy answered.

Cam tested a wrap and it appeared cool enough to touch. She picked one up and placed it on a plate with two of the cracklins and took it to her mama. "Tell us what you think, but be careful, they may still be hot." She handed her the plate and a napkin.

Camille closed her eyes and breathed in deep. "They smell delicious."

Cam took a new batch from the oil and placed it on the cutting board for Liz and Wanda to work their magic. Meanwhile, Ruth dipped out a new batch of wraps. "I have to admit, they do look good."

They all watched with anticipation as Camille picked up a wrap and took a bite, then let out a soft moan. "These are perfect, Ruth."

"Thanks, Mama." Ruth grinned.

Camille picked up a cracklin and took a bite. "Pure heaven," she said. "These are great, Cam."

"How's the spice?"

"Warm, but not too bad."

Karen and T walked up as Camille took another bite.

"Okay, girls, since Mama gives her approval, you can go ahead and take the boys a plate. Dad too," Cam said. "Eat up, ladies."

The food disappeared quickly. Cam managed to grab a cooled wrap and split in half, handing one half to Ruth. She took a bite and grinned at her friend. "Damn, you're good."

Ruth picked up a cracklin, took a bite, and smiled back at Cam. "You ain't too bad yourself."

Sandy looked up at Tab. "Please tell me you've had boudin before."

"I have now, cracklins too, and you know what? I like 'em."

Sandy shook her head and laughed. "What do folks in Monroe eat?"

"A lot of steak and chicken," Tab admitted. "Nothing that tastes this good."

Cam smiled at her lover. Tab would make a good lawyer one day. She knew exactly what to say, and when to say it, to win over a crowd.

Wanda refilled everyone's beer glasses, and the men joined the group. "Those wraps and cracklins are awesome," Buster said.

"Thanks, you've got those hogs smelling good too," Cam said.

"It's going to be a long time before they are ready. I'm thinking at least fourteen hours to get them done right, maybe longer."

"We've got plenty food to keep us from falling out until tomorrow," Camille assured them.

"There's never a doubt, Mama," Buster said. "This clan knows how to feast." He grinned and took another bite of boudin. "I sure hope you've got a recipe card for these," he said to T.

"We're up to over four hundred cards," Sandy piped up.

"Wow, you two have been busy," Tab said.

"So many great recipes to capture. I hope your caramel cake is in there." Cam smiled at her mama. "That's always been my favorite."

"It is." Sandy chuckled. "Can I tell them, Mama?"

Camille nodded to her baby. "Yes, go ahead."

"We've taken the box you bought us for the recipe cards and divided them up. Each one of us has a section of our favorite dishes Mama has made for us."

Sandy looked at her mama.

"We thought that would make it easier to find your favorites. It was Sandy's brilliant idea."

Cam pulled out the last slab of pork belly. "Great idea, Squirt." She looked over at Ruth. "You want to take a break until we start the fish and hush puppies?"

"I'll be ready whenever you are. I've forgotten how much fun cooking can be," Ruth replied. "Are these some of the fish you've been catching, Sandy?"

"They sure are."

"Sandy's done a great job of keeping our freezers stocked with filets," Camille praised.

"If nothing else, this family will never starve," Ronny chimed in.

"That's for sure. If we don't grow it, or hunt or fish for it, we barter for it." Cam smiled.

"Speaking of food, do we need to get you boys some aluminum foil to cover the meat?" Camille asked.

Ronny broke out laughing. "You won't believe what these boys have done."

"Do tell."

"Buster's taken a worn-out aluminum boat, pressure-washed it, cut it down. and welded it to the perfect size to cover the grill on the pit."

"I was wondering why you had a boat in the back of your truck," T said.

"That is genius, Buster," Camille said. "How did you come up with that?"

"I got a lot of thinking time when I'm out on the oil rigs, Mama," he answered. "My family had this old boat as an eyesore for years, so this idea allowed us to repurpose it. Jeff did most of the work on it."

"Good job, boys," Camille said with genuine appreciation.

"Thanks, Mama." Buster smiled.

The last of the wraps and cracklins had disappeared. "Should we get to cooking?" Cam asked Ruth.

"I'm ready. Let's do it."

"Do we need to carry anything out for ya?" Jeff asked.

"Sure, you can go in with the girls and they'll load you up. Thanks, Jeff."

"My pleasure." He gave Cam a bashful smile.

"Sandy, go grab your stool. I'm not sure you still need it, though, as tall as you're getting," Cam said.

When Jeff brought out the hush puppy mix, Cam began dropping spoonful-sized portions of the mixture into the hot oil as Ruth began dredging the buttermilk-soaked filets into cornmeal.

"Woohoo, I wonder what the poor people are eating tonight?" Cam crowed to the crowd. "Tonight, we're gonna eat like royalty."

"Sisters, you might want to go ahead and start the grits and set up the tables out here. Once these three get to cooking, it won't take long to fill our plates," Ronny said.

"What can we do?" Tab asked.

"You and Liz can keep my beloved company while the food and table are being prepared. The boys and I are going to baste the meat and put this fancy lid on the grill."

Sandy sat on the stool, waiting patiently until each of the hush puppies turned a golden-brown before dipping them out of the oil. Cam watched her closely to make sure the hot oil didn't burn her and saw the scar on her wrist. "Is that from the jellyfish," she asked, motioning to it.

Sandy turned her wrist over to look at it. "Yeah, but it's starting to fade."

"That seems such a long time ago, but I know it's been less than two years," Cam said.

"The best weekend of my life. I don't mind the scar. I think about our adventure every time I look at it." Sandy smiled up at her.

"We did have a great time, didn't we?"

"It was awesome. Maybe we can do it again when I graduate."

"Nope, you, baby sister, will have a special trip."

"Cam, that was special for me, because I got to spend it with you."

Cam had to look away from Sandy so she wouldn't see the tears in her eyes.

"There will be a lot of special times in your future, Sandy," Camille said. "Cherish each one like you have that trip."

Sandy smiled at her. "You can bet I will, Mama."

"Hand me one of those cooled pups, would ya, Sandy?"

Sandy stepped off her stool and took two cooled hush puppies to her mama.

"I swear, you make the best hush puppies ever," her mama said to Cam.

"Eat up; I'll keep cooking them as long as you'll eat them."

T and Wanda carried out plates and silverware and set the tables. Sauces and other condiments soon followed, along with a can of salted peanuts. Karen carried out a huge bowl of coleslaw, and a bowl of garlic grits followed as Jeff helped her carry items out. Pitchers of sweet tea and glasses of ice were brought out. When the table had a healthy mound of hush puppies and fried fish on it, Camille called her family to eat. "We better get started on this before it gets cold. Will you bless the meal for us, my love?"

"I'd love to, Mama," Ronny answered.

Cam and Ruth sat at the table and they joined hands as Ronny gave thanks for the bounty of the food, and the cooks who prepared the feast. He thanked the Lord for their wonderful growing family and friends.

When he finished, Cam placed a large mound of hush puppies and fish on the table. "We'll be done in just a few minutes and will join you then."

Cam was tickled when Tab spooned out a portion of coleslaw and poured salted peanuts on top of the mixture. "I will never eat coleslaw that doesn't come with peanuts ever again," she said after taking a bite.

Cam looked at Ruth. "See? I told you she's turned into a right nice country girl."

Her friends broke out laughing, but they couldn't argue with Cam. Tab fit in, as if she'd been born into the family.

After the feast, the group decided to let the meal settle before they tackled dessert, so Cam suggested they set off some fireworks. The pop of firecrackers had broken the silence during their meal, and what they had been concealing in the shed was much more than mere firecrackers.

Cam took a seat beside her mama and held her hand as Ruth, Liz, and Tab treated the bayou to a firework display that filled the night with beautiful colors and sights. After thirty minutes, the bayou filled with a low mist of smoke from the demonstration, and they all clapped as the final firework flared into a beautiful sunburst.

"That was fantastic, ladies," Cam said to her proud friends. The entertainment was the highlight of the night. She could even hear the cheers and catcalls from some of the neighbors who had been treated to the colorful display. "You are quite the talk of the bayou tonight," she said as they came over and took their seats.

As the smoke cleared, they looked up at the dark cloudless sky. The moon was rising, and its reflection shimmered across the water. Cam looked over at Tab, mesmerized at the sight of her. *It doesn't get much better than this.*

"Who's ready for some dessert?" Karen asked.

"I'm stuffed, but I do believe I can handle a piece of that yellow cake," Ronny told her.

"That does sound good," Cam agreed.

"Nope, not for you, big sister," Wanda said. "Caramel cake for you."

Cam's head whipped around to look at her mama.

Camille shook her head. "Not me, you can thank Karen for this one. She did it all herself."

"With your recipe of course," Karen said as she handed Cam a huge slice.

"Damn, that looks great," Liz said. "Could you be convinced to share?" she teased Cam.

Cam took a bite and moaned. "I don't know. This is way too good. I reckon you could have a little slice. Fix her up, would you, Karen? Excellent job, by the way."

Karen smiled as she continued to serve slices of the sweet desserts.

When everyone had eaten their fill and the dishes were cleared, Ronny asked, "Has anyone checked the time lately?"

Liz looked down at her watch. "Wow, we cut that close. It's five minutes until the new year."

As midnight drew closer, Ronny had them all stand and form a circle. "You better like the one you're standing next to, because at midnight you gotta kiss the people beside you," he warned.

Cam took her mama's hand in her left and Tab's in her right. After counting down the final seconds, Ronny said, "Happy New Year, everyone," and kissed Camille.

Cam leaned in to kiss Tab softly on the lips, then turned back to kiss her mama. "Happy New Year, Mama."

"Happy New Year, Cam."

They both understood this would be the last celebration they would share, and Cam's heart broke as she felt her mama's hand in hers squeezing softly.

CHAPTER NINE

Cam and her friends had arrived back at the camp around one thirty in the morning and managed to sleep in until seven. She and Tab were too exhausted from the day to make love, so Cam was content to fall asleep sandwiched between her and Willow. Willow's need to relieve her bladder woke Cam as the dog pressed her cold nose into her neck.

Yep, that will do it every time.

She crept quietly from the bed, then slipped on shorts and a T-shirt to follow an anxious Willow out the front door. "Geez, it dropped last night," Cam said to Willow, who didn't bother wasting time finding the perfect spot. She was rubbing her arms when Tab came up behind her and wrapped her arms and her thick robe around Cam.

"It got cold in the bed with you two gone," she whispered into Cam's ear. "Now I see why. Brrr, go back inside and I'll wait on Willow."

"I think she's done," Cam said as Willow raced back up the steps. "I'm sorry, but we don't have anything but a space heater out here, and I'm not even sure if that works."

"That's okay, just come back inside before you catch your death of cold."

"I'm right behind you, and ma'am, may I say that's a wonderful view."

"You are such a smooth talker, Cam St. Angelo. Go grab your robe and some slippers and I'll start the coffee."

"I beat you to it," Ruth said from her seat on the couch.

"Have I told you lately how much I love you, Ruth?" Tab joked.

"Hey now, I'm still in the room," Cam teased back. "Where did Willow go?"

"She flew past me to the bedroom, so Liz will either snuggle into her or they will both be on their way out here." Ruth laughed.

"You want to see if you can retrieve our daughter while I put on more clothes?" Cam asked Tab.

"Sure, go get warm."

"Is it that cold outside?" Ruth asked as Cam went into the bedroom.

"It's probably in the forties," Tab answered as she pulled on a thick hoodie.

"Wow, that's a big change even for the bayou. We must have had a cold front move in last night."

"You reckon," Liz said as she entered.

"I'm sorry if Willow woke you," Cam called out.

"She didn't. I was enjoying the sensual aroma of coffee. I think Willow wanted to snuggle, but the smell was too enticing."

"Aww, poor Willow," Ruth called from the couch. "Nobody for you to snuggle with?"

Cam returned to the room. "Sorry, guys, but we don't have heat in here."

"Probably not cold enough for long enough to justify it," Ruth said. "With some hot coffee, I think we'll all survive."

"You can take fresh clothes to the homestead if you want a warm shower this morning. I don't think any of us are going to be breaking a sweat today," Cam said. "I got a text that Wanda is cooking bacon and french toast for breakfast, so let's enjoy a cup of coffee and then head over for some breakfast."

"That sounds delicious," Liz said. "I can't believe I'm hungry after all we ate yesterday."

Ruth chuckled. "It's all the fresh air, my love."

"And the shivering." Tab pulled the robe tighter around her body.

Cam poured them all coffee and they sat around the small table while Willow ate her breakfast.

"She's really a good dog," Ruth said as Willow came over for petting.

"Yes, the best present I've ever gotten. She doesn't talk much, but she's good company. Loves to be out on the water too." Cam grinned.

"And loves your baby sister also," Tab reminded her.

"What's not to love about Sandy?" Liz said. "She's adorable and worships the ground you two walk on."

"I wouldn't be surprised if she turns out to be a lesbian," Cam said.

"How is Wanda holding up after Logan moved away?" Liz asked.

"It was tough at first, but honestly she's been so busy, I think it's helped keep her mind off her broken heart. Going back to school next week will probably be rough."

Ruth finished her coffee. "Drink up, my lovelies, there's french toast calling my name."

†

Cam could smell the aroma of roasting pork before they reached the homestead. "Man, that's smelling good."

"I hope the boys reconsidered sleeping outside in their sleeping bags last night," Tab said as they arrived.

"I don't see them curled up freezing. I bet Mama sent Dad out to bring them inside last night."

Tab tied off the line and they headed to the house. Willow arrived first, and Sandy met her at the door. "Here you are. We were getting hungry."

"You didn't have to wait for us, Squirt," Cam said.

"Mama said it would be impolite if we ate without you."

"Did the boys come in last night?" Cam whispered.

"Yeah, when I got up, they were curled up in their sleeping bags on the living room floor."

"Good, it got cold last night. Even the roasting pit wouldn't have been enough to keep them warm."

"You guys have it smelling good out there. We smelled it about a quarter mile away." Tab grinned when Buster came into the kitchen.

"It's coming along good. We started putting some of that applewood on it last night, and the aroma is mouthwatering," he said.

"I can attest to that," Ronny said as he entered the kitchen.

Cam frowned. "Where's Mama?"

"She's decided to sleep in for a little bit."

"Everything okay?"

Ronny nodded. "Yes, I think the late night and this change of weather is affecting her. I gave her a pain pill and will try to get her to eat something later."

"Just crack her window a little bit. If that smell doesn't make her hungry, I don't know what will," Karen said. She was cooking the french toast while T finished the bacon.

"Y'all go ahead and have a seat. I'll be bringing some food over in a second," T said.

"Anything I can help with?"

"Yes, Cam, pour juice for anyone who wants some," T answered.

She took juice orders while everyone settled around the table. Tab came into the kitchen to fill the juice order and carried full glasses to the table. "Should I put another pot of coffee on?" Tab asked.

"No, honey, I think we're good with juice and milk," Ronny answered.

"Is there any of that coleslaw left from last night?" Tab asked.

"Eww, for breakfast?" Sandy said.

"No, silly, to go with dinner. It was so good, it's got me craving more."

"Man, that's a relief." Cam chuckled.

"Don't worry, Tab, we've got another huge bowl that hasn't even been touched yet," Karen assured her.

"Somebody got the peas soaking yet?" Cam asked.

"Taken care of," T said.

"What kind of peas?" Tab innocently asked and all heads turned to look at her.

Cam just shook her head. "Oh boy, I guess I'm going to have to take your country-girl badge away from you. You've never had Hoppin' John?"

"Hopping who?"

"Hoppin' John, spicy black-eyed peas over white rice. It's a New Year's tradition to eat it to bring in good luck," Cam explained.

"Nope, never heard of it."

Sandy smacked her head. "Man, I thought there was hope for Tab."

The others at the table broke out laughing. "No worry, Squirt, there's still hope," Cam assured her.

"But, but, we had pizza last year when we went back to school. Back me up here, Ruth," she implored.

"That was for dinner. We'd already had our peas at lunch. I'm sorry, my friend."

"Well dang, I guess there's a new tradition on my horizon. Is there anything else I should know about for today?"

"Whatever you do today, you'll be doing all year long," Ronny said.

"So eating great food with family and great friends it is." Tab smiled.

"Now we're talking," Sandy said.

"Is there anything you need us to do today to get ready?" Cam asked.

"I think we've got everything under control, honey," Ronny answered. "The inside food's pretty much ready and the hogs are cooking nicely. Is there something you wanted to do?"

"If it warms up a bit, I think I'll give the ladies the tour of the bayou," Cam answered.

Sandy's head popped up from her plate.

"Yes, you can come along." Cam beat her to the punch, then heard a cough from the bedroom. "I'll be right back."

She walked down the hall to the master bedroom and peeked inside. Her mama was sitting on the edge of the bed, holding a bloodied tissue. She balled the tissue in her hand as she desperately tried to hide it when she saw Cam standing there.

Cam rushed into the room. "Mama, are you okay?"

Camille nodded. "Just a bloody nose," she answered. "I'm fine."

Cam knew better, but she wasn't going to question her. "The girls cooked french toast and bacon. Will you try to eat some?"

"No bacon, but a piece of french toast and some apple juice sounds good."

Cam smiled. "I'll be right back."

She returned to the kitchen and cut up a slice of french toast. "Sandy, if you're done will you pour Mama a glass of apple juice?"

"I'll bring it right down."

Cam grabbed a napkin and went down the hallway, leaving her breakfast untouched.

†

Ronny saw Tab's brow wrinkle with concern and watched her stand up. "Stay and finish. I'm done. I'll send Cam back to eat."

He followed Sandy down the hall.

Cam was sitting on the edge of the bed beside her mama, and Sandy had placed the glass of juice beside the bed before returning to the kitchen. He looked at Cam. "You go eat breakfast and I'll keep your mama company."

"It's okay, Dad, I don't mind."

"I know you don't, but you need to eat. I need you to stay strong."

Cam must have heard the pleading in his words because she nodded and stood to return to the kitchen. "Just call if you need anything."

"I've got two perfectly good legs. Now go and eat."

"Yes, sir," she said and left the bedroom.

†

"Come sit, I've made you some fresh," Karen said as she slid two pieces of french toast onto a plate. "Is there enough bacon left?"

"There will be if I move it out of Ruth's reach," Liz teased her lover. She passed the plate to Cam as the others started cleaning the kitchen.

†

When they left the camp, Sandy and Willow were the first to reach the boat, and Sandy untied the line, waiting for the others to board.

"Thanks, Squirt." Cam stepped onto the boat and turned to take Tab's hand. "I'm glad it's starting to warm up a bit."

185

"Me too, I wasn't expecting to step outside into the cold this morning." Tab took a seat beside Cam.

"Where are we gonna go first, Cam?" Sandy coiled the rope and slipped into the boat.

"I thought we'd head far south and work our way back. See what we can see this morning." Cam started the motor.

"As cool as it is, there should be a lot of movement from warm-blooded creatures trying to stay warm and eat." Sandy slid into a seat beside Liz and hugged Willow.

"See how smart she's getting. I swear she knows the bayou better than anyone." Cam smiled at her kid sister and pulled away from the dock.

Cam was thankful for the light jacket she'd grabbed on her way out of the house. The sun had finally burned through the fog, but the breeze as the boat moved across the water still held a brisk chill. She looked over at Tab and smiled when she saw that her lover had drawn her hands inside the sleeves of her sweatshirt to keep them warm. Liz and Ruth took the more traditional route and snuggled close together. Only Sandy seemed to be unaffected by the chill. Her light blond hair blew back from her face as she scanned the water for signs of life.

Cam aimed for the southern slough that bordered their property. She and Sandy often spotted a nesting pair of ospreys in the top of an ancient cypress tree, and she slowed to enter the slough. The one Cam thought was the male took flight from the nest and flew overhead as their eyes followed his path.

Tab looked at Cam. "Was that an eagle?"

"They are called ospreys but are also known as sea eagles or fish eagles."

"That looked like the male leaving the nest. I bet he was going in search of breakfast," Sandy said.

"I bet you're right. I think that pair has made this slough home for about ten years, since you were born, Squirt."

Sandy smiled back at Cam. "They eat fish, snakes, and frogs; just about anything they can catch on the water."

Cam spotted a nutria swimming ahead of them and pointed out to Tab. "That's a nutria, or a swamp rat as we call them. They were originally brought in for their fur when other fur-bearing animals started getting trapped out, but the quality of their coats wasn't up to par. The damned things breed like rabbits and in some places have to be hunted to cull the population."

"What are they good for?" Tab asked.

"Gator food, mostly. The gators seem to enjoy them for a snack. The meat's tough and gamey, so we don't bother with them," Sandy replied.

"Do you think we'll see Bubba Gump today?" Tab said as she looked at Sandy.

"He's probably dug in somewhere trying to get warm. If the sun comes out bright, he may decide to sun himself," she explained.

"To hear Tab talk about him, he sounds like he's about thirty feet long." Ruth elbowed her friend.

"Not quite, but he is the biggest gator in these parts, pushing closer to fifteen feet, I'd guess," Cam replied.

"Do you think I could go on a hunt with you sometime?" Ruth asked.

"You could come down on a weekend during the season and I'll put you to work." Cam winked. "It normally runs mid-September through mid-October here."

"I'd like that."

"Just make sure she comes back with all her fingers and toes," Liz warned.

"I'll keep her safe, I promise, Liz."

Sandy pointed out a large blue heron as it strolled awkwardly through the shallow water along the banks. "Another fisher," she said as the bird's head disappeared under the water, then emerged with a small fish in its beak.

"You have a lot of competition for the fish here, don't ya?" Liz asked.

"I do, but the fish fear me most," Sandy laughed.

"Hey, I have a shirt that says that." Tab grinned.

"You've turned into a great fisherwoman," Cam replied.

"That's because I had a great teacher." Tab smiled at Sandy.

"Yes, ma'am, you did," Cam agreed as she pulled the boat onto the bank. "Tie us off, will you, Squirt?"

"Sure, but where are we going?"

"We may have a surprise this morning, but everyone is going to have to be very quiet."

Sandy leapt onto shore and wrapped the line around a tree, and Willow jumped from the boat to sit beside her. After Cam got everyone off the boat safely, she pulled it higher on the bank and tied the rope snuggly around the trunk.

"Very quietly now," she whispered as she took Tab's hand and crept through the underbrush. "Keep an eye on Willow."

As they reached a small clearing, Cam stopped and pointed across to the feeder they had set up. A doe and her set of twins were eating the sweet feed she had left for them. She knelt so her friends could see.

Sandy's eyes met Cam's, sparkling with excitement.

Willow had followed them off the boat and sat beside Sandy. When her eyes caught the movement, she let out a short woof.

Sandy grabbed her collar before she could launch after the deer. "Shh, Willow," she commanded, but it was too late. The doe had scented them and bolted for cover with her twins right behind her.

"Sorry, Cam," Sandy said.

"No problem. I'm glad y'all got a glimpse of them. Aren't they adorable?" She smiled at Tab, who was smiling up at her.

"They really are. I could just love all over them," Tab replied.

"I've been seeing them pretty often since they were born and thought they may be out here feeding this morning. We got lucky."

Sandy grinned up at Cam. "I'd say so."

They returned to the boat and continued their tour. Sandy pointed out a log full of sunning turtles, and several more species of wading birds for the group. They only saw one gator on the banks of a slough, so Ruth and Liz would have to wait for another trip to meet Bubba Gump.

When they were in sight of the homestead, there was a flurry of activity in the backyard as people rushed to get food and dishes ready for the feast. The lid was off the pit, and the hogs were a glistening golden-brownish red.

"I can taste it now," she told Tab.

"It smells heavenly," Tab said and the growling of her stomach accented her comment.

"Let's go see what we need to do to help," Liz said as they pulled up to the dock.

Sandy had them tied off before she and Willow rushed across the yard to join her dad and the boys inspecting the hogs.

"Those look delicious," she said. Willow sat beside her, licking her chops.

"The smaller one is ready, so we're gonna pull him off the fire to let him cool," Buster told her.

"Your mama and the girls should have the rest of the food pretty close to ready. Why don't you see if you can go ahead and set the outdoor tables for her?" Ronny suggested.

"Yes, sir." Sandy spun away and nearly ran into Cam as her sister walked up behind them.

"Slow your roll, little sister. That looks like good eatin'," she told the boys.

"Don't look like anyone's gonna go hungry today," Ronny said. "You should see the kitchen. It's full of food."

"How's Mama?"

"Sitting like a queen on the throne, handing out orders left and right. The girls won't let her do anything else."

"That's good. I'll go see if they need any help."

†

They spent the entire afternoon and well into evening eating. So much food was left that Ronny didn't know what they'd do with all the leftovers.

"Leave that to me," Buster said and pulled out his cell phone. He walked away from the group and made several short calls. When he returned he wore a huge grin, "Help's on the way."

Moments later, the air filled with sirens and a fire truck and two parish sheriff squad cars pulled into the front yard.

"You literally meant help was on the way," Ronny said.

"What better folks to feed than our volunteer fire fighters, and the deputies that protect us?" Buster grinned and walked over to meet the approaching crew.

"That will certainly take care of the worry about storing leftovers," Camille said as six male deputies and one female deputy approached.

"Let me grab some extra plates," Cam said and rushed back into the house.

The family moved from the table to the lawn chairs to free up space for the arriving guests. They took seats around the table and smiled at all the food.

"This certainly beats the heck out of your spaghetti, Tommy Joe," one of the fireman said.

The St. Angelos and friends had finished off the smaller hog but had barely broken into the larger hog.

"This is leftovers?" one of the officers said. "I can't imagine what the full meal looked like."

"Pretty much the same, Bobby, just lots more of it. We've been eating for hours," Buster said.

"That's mighty fine of y'all to invite us to eat," the captain of the fire squad said.

"Everyone deserves to start off the New Year with a hearty meal," Camille told him.

"Well, this certainly qualifies, ma'am. Thank you."

"Thank you. I was starting to worry where we were going to put all the leftovers. Y'all eat what you can and we'll send you back with plates for later," Camille said.

Ruth got up from her chair and pulled some of the meat off the hog to fill a small plate. When she took her seat beside Liz, she smiled. "That's why they call it a pig pickin', darlin, you can't help but keep picking at it all night it tastes so danged good." She popped a morsel into her mouth and grinned.

"She's one hundred percent right, Liz. The bigger the hog, the longer the pickin' goes on. I'm not sure even with the extra help we'll manage to eat that entire big boy," Ronny said.

"If not, it'll make for some great pulled-pork sandwiches tomorrow. You can bet me and the boys will take a break from working on the house to come eat some of them for you." Buster grinned.

†

It was almost ten before they made it back to the camp. Ruth groaned as she stepped off the boat and looked up at Cam. "I think I'm gonna die, I ate so much."

"Naw, you'll be hollering you're hungry again by midnight," Cam said.

"It's probably a good thing Karen hooked us up with a big platter of meat and a couple loaves of bread, then," Tab said as she handed Cam the cooler.

"They will make a great lunch after we go four wheeling tomorrow." Cam offered Tab her hand to steady her in the dark as she climbed from the boat.

Willow trotted ahead of them, and even the young pup acted sluggish from all the food. Tab took the cooler from Cam and led the others inside while Cam sat on the steps to wait on Willow. Moments later, the door creaked open and Ruth came out.

"You doing okay?" she asked as she sat beside her.

"Yeah, I'm just worried about Mama. She's started having nosebleeds. She didn't look good to me today," Cam admitted.

"There's been a lot of activity out here the last few days. Hopefully that's just got her worn down. After we leave tomorrow, and after the holidays are done for a while, things will settle back down," Ruth said as she slung her arm around Cam's shoulders. "Is there anything I can do for you, my friend?"

"Just pray that when she goes, it will be quick and pain-free," Cam said as she wiped her eyes.

"I can do that. I pray for y'all every day. I just wish there was something I could do to ease your pain."

"Not unless you have a miracle cure up your sleeve."

"I wish I did, Cam, truly I do."

Willow came rushing back to her and licked the tears from Cam's face, and Ruth scratched her head. "You might think I'm crazy, and I wouldn't blame you if you did, but I think Willow has been sent to be a guardian angel for this family."

"She's been great for all of us," Cam admitted.

"Even your dad was sneaking bites of food to her under the table today."

Cam laughed. "I missed that."

"Numerous times, might I add. I think she's probably as miserable as I am right now. I think I'm going to round up my honey and go to bed."

"Sounds good. I'll walk in with you." Cam stood and stretched before entering the cabin.

"See y'all for breakfast," Cam said and wished her friends good night. When they left the room, she turned to

Tab and sighed. "I am so ready to get out of these clothes and lie down."

"I know I say this after every meal, but that was one of the best meals of my life." Tab took Cam's hand and led her into the bedroom. She waited for Willow and then closed the door behind them.

"It was great food. I'm so glad y'all were here to share it with us," Cam said as she began stripping. "You want to rinse off in the shower with me? I smell like smoke." She sniffed and wrinkled her nose.

"That's not a bad idea." Tab followed her into the bathroom.

After the shower, they made love slowly until both women were content, then fell asleep wrapped in each other's arms.

†

After a light breakfast, the four friends spent the morning in the Gator, and Cam took them deep into the property, hitting every mud puddle and bog she could find. They laughed and had a carefree morning. When they returned to the camp, they were all covered with mud.

They showered, and Cam tossed their muddy clothing in the washer while Liz and Tab made sandwiches for lunch.

"Oh, my goodness. I would have never dreamed that this meat could taste any better, but it's even more delicious today," Ruth said as she made a second sandwich.

"If those feral hogs keep producing like they have we'll be hunting every few months to thin them down before they trash the entire island," Cam said. "Come down and we'll go hunting and get Tony at LB's to process the meat for you."

"That does sound tempting. I haven't hunted in ages," Ruth replied.

"You're always welcome."

"I'm almost afraid to ask what the family has planned for tonight," Tab said.

Cam chuckled. "A light meal, for a change."

"Good, I feel like I've gained twenty pounds since we've been here," Liz said.

"Ha! Don't worry, Coach will work them off you," Tab said.

"I don't miss that part of training," Cam said.

"Who are you kidding? You were always the first to finish your workouts," Ruth said.

"Just to keep y'all motivated." Cam grinned.

"You did that well," Ruth said. "I hope you can make some games and maybe the conference tournament. It's in Tuscaloosa this year."

"I'll try my best," Cam promised. "Sandy is already asking to go to games, so that will be incentive for us to finish our chores early in the week."

"You're more than welcome anytime. Sandy can stay with Ruth and me to give y'all some private time too."

"That would be really nice."

CHAPTER TEN

Cam hated to see her friends leave early the next day, but they had to prepare for classes and to resume practice to be prepared to play ball. The season would be starting soon, and they would be playing almost every weekend until the tournaments started.

After they drove off, Cam sighed deeply. She'd love to be going back with them, but her family needed her more. Her mama hadn't been able to see them off, so each had visited with her privately before they left. Their eyes were filled with tears as they climbed into Tab's car.

"Call if there's anything we can do," Ruth had said as she hugged Cam and climbed into the passenger seat.

"I'll call you tonight," Tab said with a forced smile. "Love you."

"Love you more. Be careful."

"We will."

Cam watched her friends drive away, then called Willow to her and returned inside.

†

Camille spent most of the day in bed, and the medications did little to ease the pain that ran rampant through her body. Her appetite was gone and she struggled to keep liquids down. Cam looked at her dad sitting across the bed from her, and his concern mirrored her own. "Is it time to go to the hospital, Mama?"

"No, Cam, I promise I'll be better tomorrow. I just need to sleep and I'll be better. I'm not ready to go, Cam," she implored.

"All right, Mama. I trust you to let us know when it gets too much for you."

"I will. I just want to sleep now."

"I'll stay with her for a bit," Ronny said. "Go stretch your legs."

Cam left the master bedroom and stormed straight outside. Willow, playing on the living room floor with Sandy, rushed to follow her. Sandy stood up to follow, but Wanda stopped her. "Give her a bit of time." Cam heard her call to Sandy. She was relieved when no one but Willow followed her outside.

Cam walked to the water's edge and knelt. She could no longer fight back the tears she had worked so hard for weeks to conceal. Her body was racked with sobs as she cried for her mama's pain, her pain, and the pain the family was going through.

"It just isn't fucking fair," she said when Willow sat beside her. Cam leaned over to hug the pup, and Willow's soft tongue caressed her cheek, licking away her salty tears. "You must be my guardian angel." She hugged Willow tightly again.

Cam ran her sleeve over her face to dry her eyes, then stood and walked over to the boat to cross over to the camp. When she went into the cabin, she packed a bag with several outfits and hygiene products. It was time for her to move back into the house. She decided to sleep on the couch to keep from disrupting her sisters but doubted she would get much sleep in the coming days. She felt deep inside her soul that her mama's time was near. She grabbed a full bag of Willow's dog food and locked the cabin behind her.

Sandy and Wanda were sitting under the pavilion when she returned. They rushed to meet her at the dock and helped her with the bags. Her heart nearly broke when she looked at her young sister's eyes.

"Mama's time is getting close, isn't it?" Wanda asked.

She nodded. "Yeah, I think so. I think she was hanging on for one more holiday with us, but she's grown so weary."

Sandy dropped the bag of dog food and rushed to cling to Cam. Cam knelt and pulled them both close. "Everything's going to be okay. It will be tough at first, but we'll make it through this together. Don't ever forget how much I love you."

"We love you too," Wanda sniffled.

"I'm going to move back into the house, but I'm gonna sleep on the couch. I don't think I'll be getting much sleep anyhow."

"You can have my bed, Cam," Wanda offered.

"Thanks, but Squirt snores too much," she said to tease a smile from her baby sister.

"Nuh-uh, Cam, you're the one who snores."

"Who do you think I learned from?" She ruffled Sandy's hair and hugged her close. "I'm fine on the couch but thank you."

When they walked into the house, Ronny was just hanging up the phone. He looked as bad as Cam felt.

"I just called her nurse to come early," he said. "She's sleeping for now."

"Anything we can do?" Cam asked.

"I wish I knew. Just keep everyone fed. Try to keep them busy."

"I'll do my best," she promised.

He nodded and walked back to the bedroom to sit with his beloved.

†

Cam called the girls to sit around the table and explained to them as best she could that their mama was starting to fade. "Her Hospice nurse should be arriving shortly to examine her. T, I want you to come for me when she arrives, please."

"Where will you be?" Karen asked.

"Wanda and Sandy are going to help me get some mash started."

Karen nodded. "What can we do?"

"You and T can get lunch ready and work out something for supper. Some cookies would be nice too." Cam forced a smile. "Mama may need to go to the hospital soon. Dad and I will probably take turns sitting with her.

199

We're going to need y'all to work together to keep the house clean and each other fed. No junk food, either," she teased. "School starts back for y'all Monday. Are you all set?"

"I think we're all good," T said.

"Do we have to go if Mama's in the hospital?" Wanda asked.

"We'll have to play it by ear and see how things go. You know Mama wouldn't want you to miss school." Cam looked at their sad faces. "Any questions?" When none of them spoke, Cam said, "Let's get to work then. Love y'all."

†

Cam, Wanda, Sandy, and Willow walked out to the shed, and Cam inspected the mash barrels. "Will you two take these outside and rinse them thoroughly?"

"You got it, Cam. Come on, Squirt." Wanda grabbed the first of the large barrels.

Cam surveyed the shelves to make sure she had the yeast and other ingredients she'd need to start the mash, then began to chop the cane stalks into smaller pieces. Several new bags of dried corn were stacked in the bed of the small trailer.

The door opened and her sisters returned with the first two barrels, freshly rinsed, and carried out the next two. Cam opened a bag of corn, poured it into a barrel, and moved to the next. She would prepare three for corn mash and two for cane. She poured yeast and the other mixtures into the barrels, then resumed cutting the cane sections. When they finished rinsing the barrels, Cam got Sandy started filling them with water while Wanda helped her finish cutting the cane.

They were nearly finished with the cane when T came to let Cam know the nurse had arrived. She gave them instructions and left the shed.

When she walked into the bedroom, the nurse looked up at her with worry in her eyes. She finished her examination and sat on the bed next to Camille. Cam and Ronny moved closer to the bed, and Cam took her mama's hand as the nurse began to talk.

"I wish I had better news for you, Camille, but your body is beginning to shut down. The swelling is from your kidneys, which have stopped working. Have you voided at all today?"

"A very little, but early this morning," Camille answered.

"Have you eaten anything?"

"A bowl of grits this morning."

"How is your pain?"

"It's always there. I can't seem to get comfortable."

"Are you taking your pain meds?"

"Like clockwork," Ronny answered. "I'm not sure if they help her much."

"I can give her a shot of something stronger, but that's all I can do to make her more comfortable here. You need to consider going to the hospital where they can keep you hydrated and give you stronger medications to ease your pain."

"Maybe tomorrow," Camille answered.

"Fair enough. Let me get an injection ready for you, then."

The nurse stepped away from the bed to draw from a vial of medication, then administered the shot. She placed the used syringe in her bag and turned back to them. "You have my number if you need to call. Don't hesitate," she said as she touched Ronny's arm gently.

"I'll walk out with you. Be right back," Cam said and walked the nurse out to her car. "Is there anything else you can share with me?" she asked when they were outside.

The nurse smiled weakly. "She's getting close to crossing over, and she needs to go to the hospital sooner rather than later. I'll be out early in the morning to check on her unless you need me tonight. If she hasn't improved significantly, I'm going to insist she goes in. They can make it easier for all of you."

"Any idea of how long?" Cam's voice cracked.

"It's impossible to tell. Your mama seems like a fighter, but her body has given up on her. Two days, maybe longer, but I wouldn't count on more. She seems more tired than I've ever seen her."

"I think she was just trying to share one last holiday with us," Cam admitted.

"You are probably right about that. Call if there's any change, good or bad, please. Take care of yourselves too. It's going to be hard on all of you."

"Thanks," Cam said and closed the door behind her. She walked back to check on her mama.

Ronny looked up when she entered the room. "Whatever she gave her was strong. She's sleeping."

"Can we go outside and talk?"

"Sure thing, honey." He stood and followed Cam from the room.

"Keep an ear out for Mama," she said to T as they walked past.

Outside, they took seats around the fire pit. "What's on your mind, honey?"

"The nurse thinks Mama will only last another two days, or so. She can't be sure, but I think, regardless, Mama needs to go to the hospital tomorrow. She'll be more comfortable there than we can provide here."

"I agree," he said to Cam's relief.

"I know she's sleeping now, but if she's more alert later, I think we all need some time alone with her to say our goodbyes. I don't want anyone to miss out on that chance."

"That's true. Anything else?"

"When she goes to the hospital, you and I need to rotate shifts sitting with her. Neither one of us can do this alone. I'll take the nights, if you can sit with her during the daytime. I'll make sure the girls have everything they need."

A tear slid down his cheek. "Thanks for being here, Cam. I couldn't do this alone."

"We'll get through this, Dad. Our family is strong, and we'll pull together."

"I know, honey."

Cam pulled him into a tight embrace. "I think the girls have made some sandwiches for lunch. Let's go eat, and I'll pull them together to talk afterward while you sit with Mama."

Ronny nodded, and they returned inside to find the girls had made tuna fish sandwiches. "Man, that's a relief. I think I'm burned out on pork for a while."

"It sure was good, but next time we'll cook smaller hogs." Cam bit into a sandwich. "Hey, T, do we have any of those sweet baby gherkins?"

"I think so. Hang on I'll check."

T brought a large jar of pickles to the table.

"You're in luck," Wanda said. "Grab some and pass them this way, please."

"What? I have to share?" Cam grinned.

"Yes, you do, so pass your sister the pickles," Ronny said. "Then I want them, Wanda."

"Go ahead, Dad, another minute or two isn't going to kill me."

"You want these?" Cam asked as she offered him the jar, then pulled them back. She winked at Karen. "Karen, will you pass the pickles to Dad?"

"Sure, Cam." She took the jar from Cam and winked at T. "T, will you pass these pickles to Dad?"

T took the pickles and walked to the other end of the table. "I won't be mean, Dad," she said and handed him the jar.

"Spoilsport." Cam winked at T.

†

After they had cleaned up from lunch, Cam sat with her sisters around the table and explained what was happening with their mama. They received the news as bravely as they could, but Cam understood their devastation and despair. Sandy crawled into her lap for comfort and laid her head on Cam's shoulder.

"It's important that we all have some special time with Mama as soon as we can. Her pain is getting worse, and the stronger medications will make it difficult for her to hold a conversation for long periods when she goes to the hospital."

"She'll go tomorrow, is that right?" Karen said.

"Yes, tonight if she gets worse," Cam shared. "When she goes, Dad will go with her. The rest of us will go up for a visit, then Dad will come home with y'all and I'll spend the night with Mama." She looked at Karen. "I really need you to step up and help Dad make sure everyone is ready for school on Monday."

"I will." Karen nodded.

"It's going to take all of us working together. Sandy, can I trust you'll care for Willow when I'm not here?"

"Yes, of course. I love Willow."

"I know you do, sweetie, and she loves you."

Cam looked around the table at her sisters' solemn faces. "You know what I'd like for supper?"

T looked up. "What, Cam?"

"A huge breakfast. With the works. Sausage, bacon, ham, with some of those scrambled eggs with cheese you cook so well, Karen. Could you make some homemade hash browns, and biscuits, T?"

Sandy raised her head to look at Cam. "What can I make?"

"Mama loves grits, so how about grits and toast?"

"I can do that." Sandy smiled.

"I'll make some sausage gravy too," Cam told them. "Nobody beats my sausage gravy."

Karen nodded. "That's for sure."

Cam smiled at them. "We can start around five. Is that good for everyone?"

"Sounds like a feast is in order," T said. "I've got a few loads of clothing to catch up on."

"Bring them out when they're dry, and we can help fold them. I'm going to start on a shopping list. We're getting low on a few things," Karen said.

"If you put that together, Sandy and I can go shopping before supper. Would you mind helping me?" Cam looked at Wanda. "Two carts would make it go faster."

Wanda perked up. "We can finish in no time."

"Finish your list and I'll check with Dad to see if he needs anything." Cam sat Sandy on her feet and left the room.

When she walked into her parents' room, her dad was sitting beside the bed watching Camille sleep. "Everyone is busy doing chores and getting ready to make a big breakfast for supper. I'm taking Squirt and Wanda to help me grocery shop. Is there anything you need?"

"Not that I can think of, honey. You know where the checkbook is, right?"

"Yes, Dad, we've got everything under control. We'll be back soon. I've got my phone if anything comes up."

Ronny nodded and turned his attention back to Camille.

Cam was walking down the hall when her cell phone vibrated in her pocket. She pulled it out and saw Tab's number on the screen. "Hang on one second," she told Tab when she answered and walked out to the front porch. "Hey there." She listened for several seconds. "It's been a busy afternoon; sorry I missed your first call. Mama's not doing well. We're going to take her to the hospital tomorrow if things don't change tonight. No, honey, I don't know of anything you can do." She smiled. "Yes, prayers would be much appreciated. Dad will stay with her during the day and I'll sit with her at night. … No, thanks for offering, but don't come down."

Cam ran her fingers through her hair. "You're always with me, baby. Yes, I'll keep you posted. I'm taking the two young ones to town to grocery shop. Everyone is hanging in there. … Yes, I'll tell them. Goodbye for now. … Love you more."

She walked inside to find her sisters sitting around the table discussing meals and supplies. "Don't forget about washing detergent, toilet paper, hygiene stuff," she said as she walked to the fridge for a bottle of water. "Stuff for school lunches, or do y'all eat at the cafeteria?"

"Eeeww, yuck," Wanda said. "The only decent meal is the fried chicken on Wednesday."

"Better plan on lunchmeat, then. Fresh bread too."

"If you'll pick up ingredients, I'll make some rice-crispy treats and cookies to pack in lunches," T said.

"That almost makes me want to be back in school," Cam teased. "Add a bag of puppy chow and some treats for the mutt, please."

"Okay, I think I've got everything." Karen passed the list to Cam.

"Let's go, compadres. Will you keep an eye on Willow for me? Where is Willow?"

"In bed with Mama," T said as she walked down the hall.

Smiling, Cam walked out of the house with her sisters in tow.

†

With the groceries put away, they focused on making supper. Camille was awake and sitting against the headboard when Cam walked down to check on her parents.

"Breakfast is almost ready, Mama. What do you think you could eat? We have grits, scrambled eggs, every meat you can imagine, hash browns, biscuits, gravy, and toast."

"Make a bowl for me if you would, Cam. Open a biscuit and put it on the bottom, with scrambled eggs, grits, hash browns, and some of your gravy on top."

"No meat, Mama?"

"No, I don't think my stomach can handle it right now."

"I'll make Mama's bowl and come sit with her while you go eat, Dad."

"I'm okay, Cam."

"Go eat. Cam and I'll be just fine," Camille said.

"All right, then," he conceded.

"Apple juice, Mama?"

"That's perfect."

"I'll be right back."

"Pour Mama some apple juice and take it to her please, Squirt, while I fix her bowl," she said as she reentered the kitchen. The girls crowded around Cam as she fixed the bowl her mama had requested.

"That actually looks pretty good," Wanda said.

"Yeah, it does, doesn't it?" Cam smiled. "Make one for yourself and join Mama and me."

Cam carried the bowl in to her mama and sent her dad to eat. She handed the bowl to Camille and sat on the end of the bed. "Made with love," she promised.

"Like every meal we've ever shared." Camille smiled as she picked up the spoon.

"Wanda is going to join us in a few minutes."

"That's good, Cam, and so is this bowl."

"Eat what you can, and if there's anything else you want just let us know."

"I will, honey. Thank you."

†

For the next few hours, the girls took turns going in to talk with their mama. She managed to finish the bowl but declined seconds. Cam joined her dad for a meal, surrounded by her sisters, and then they cleaned the kitchen.

When T returned from the bedroom, she looked at her dad. "Mama says she's ready to sleep now."

Ronny looked at Cam. "You got this?"

"Yes, sir, we do. Go retire with Mama."

Cam and the girls spent the evening playing cards around the kitchen table while fresh cookies baked in the oven. As the hour grew late, Cam stood and stretched. "I'm going to take Willow outside, then crash on the couch. Y'all need to get ready for bed. Tomorrow is going to be a long day."

Each of her sisters gave Cam a hug and a kiss before going down the hall to their rooms. Cam watched them go and followed Willow out the back door. Cam sat in a chair around the fire pit while Willow explored. The moon had risen and the reflection shimmering across the water was beautiful. The crickets chirped and bullfrogs croaked in the distance. It was such a perfect, peaceful night outside, much different from the storm of emotion roiling inside the house.

She listened to the music of the bayou until her head snapped up, and Cam realized she had drifted off. She turned her head and found Willow lying beside her. "Let's go see if we can get some sleep, girl," she said and they went inside.

Cam changed clothes and walked quietly down the hall to look in on her parents. Camille was wrapped in Ronny's arms, and a smile of contentment played across both their faces. She sighed softly, knowing the smiles would soon fade. Cam then returned to the living room and stretched out on the couch. Willow hopped up beside her, and Cam snuggled into her warmth as she pulled a light blanket over them.

She concentrated on the ticking of the mantel clock until her eyes grew heavy and she drifted on a sea of memories.

†

Cam jolted awake around five when she sensed movement and she quickly walked to her parents' room. Ronny was helping Camille into a sweater. He looked up at Cam with worry-filled eyes.

"It's time to go," he said. "Will you bring my truck up close and help me with your mama?"

"Yes, sir," she answered and rushed back to tuck her shirt in her jeans and slip into a pair of shoes. She was so exhausted last night, she didn't bother undressing. Willow followed her outside as Cam started her dad's truck and pulled it up next to the porch.

She opened the passenger door and returned inside. When she entered the bedroom, Ronny scooped up Camille in his arms and carried her from the house. She had never been a big woman, but the ease with which he carried her told Cam just how much weight her mama had lost.

"Catch the doors for me, Cam."

Cam ran ahead to open the front door and followed them out to the truck. "Call the nurse and give her an update, please, so she doesn't come out unnecessarily."

"I will."

"I'll call you when we get settled into a room. You can bring the girls up later for a visit."

"Is there anything else I need to do?"

"Yes, give your mama a kiss," Camille answered from inside the truck.

Cam rushed over to her and hugged her gently. "Love you, Mama."

"I love you too. Be careful and I'll see you soon." Camille forced a smile, then winced.

"Love you too, Dad. Be safe. I'll wait for your call."

Cam watched them drive away and went inside to start a pot of coffee. It was sure to be a long day. She poured a cup and took it outside to watch the sun rise across the bayou. A beautiful Sunday sky lit the horizon, and the water was remarkably free of mist or fog on such a cool morning. She hoped wherever her mama was, she was seeing the beautiful sunrise.

Her phone vibrated in her pocket, and she pulled it out to see a text from Tab.

I woke up suddenly with you on my mind. Is everything okay?

Mama just left for the hospital. I'll text or call later, okay?

I'm here, and I love you.

Love you too.

†

When she walked back inside for a refill, she met T in the kitchen and was startled by the terror in her eyes.

"What's going on Cam?"

"Mama's gone to the hospital. Throw some clothes on and join me for some coffee outside until the others get up."

Cam poured another cup and returned to watch the bayou as it came alive. She made a quick call to the nurse to inform her that Camille had gone to the hospital and thanked her for her kind care. T pulled up a chair beside her as she ended the call.

"Dad took Mama to the hospital just a little while ago. As soon as she gets settled into a room and is ready for visitors, he will give me a call and I'll take everyone over."

T nodded and took a sip of her coffee as she gazed across the bayou. "Beautiful, isn't it?"

"As it will always be," Cam answered.

When the others woke, Cam let them know what had happened. "Get dressed and I'll warm up the biscuits and gravy so when Dad calls, we'll be ready."

Cam showered quickly and dressed in fresh clothes. She was warming the biscuits when Karen arrived.

"What can I do?"

"Set out some plates and pour some juice," Cam answered.

The atmosphere around the breakfast table was somber. Cam nearly jumped out of her skin when the house phone rang, and she rushed to answer.

"Sorry, honey, I couldn't remember your cell phone number."

"No problem, Dad. How's Mama?"

"Resting now. She's in room 214. Bring the girls up when you can. She's in some pain, so she's sleeping off and on, but she'll want to see her babies."

"We'll see you in just a few minutes." She hung up. "Willow, you need to stay and be a good girl," she said when the pup started to whine. "Not this time," Cam gave her an awkward smile.

"I'll call Buster. He can take her over to the house and keep an eye on her," T said.

"Great idea. Thanks. We'll wait for you in the Jeep."

CHAPTER ELEVEN

The day passed all too quickly. When Camille said she was tired after a late lunch, Cam looked at Ronny.

"Take the girls home and let them prepare supper. I'll call if anything changes," she said.

Ronny was hesitant to leave, but Camille insisted he go home to rest and promised she'd see him in the morning.

Reluctantly he kissed her lips and led the girls from the room.

Cam settled into a reclining chair beside her bed and reached out to cover her mama's hand. Her arms had IV lines taped down to her skin, but Camille took Cam's hand in hers and gave it a gentle squeeze. Cam remembered how cool her skin had been recently, even when the room was comfortably warm. Camille rested against her pillows and drifted off to sleep.

The sound of her mama's heartbeat on the monitor lulled Cam to sleep.

Cam woke hours later when the air swooshed from the door closing. She was disoriented for a second, until she remembered she was in the hospital. A heavenly smell reached her senses, and she looked over to find a foil-covered plate with a note taped to it.

I heard about Mama and I knew you'd be here. Brought your favorite. Call if you need anything. Love ya. B

Cam smiled at her best friend from high school's sweet note. Beside the plate was a Mountain Dew bottle, which Cam opened and took a long sip from. The foil covering the plate was still warm as she peeled it back to find a fried boneless chicken breast, rice, gravy, and cut corn. She hadn't thought she was hungry, but the food smelled too good to resist. Bren had turned into a great cook. Cam filled her stomach with the delicious meal, then drifted back to sleep.

When she woke next, just after two in the morning, Camille was watching her.

"Hey, Mama. How are you feeling?"

"I'm okay, Cam. I wish you'd go home and sleep in a real bed."

"I'm fine right here. Bren brought me a great dinner, so I don't need anything at all."

"She's always been a good friend to you."

"Yes, she has. She's turned into a good cook too." Cam smiled.

"You're not too bad yourself, young lady."

"I had great teachers."

"I couldn't ask for a better daughter. I know the family will be in good hands when I'm gone."

"I promise I'll do my best, Mama."

Camille smiled. "I know you will, honey."

Cam took her hand. "Is there anything I can do for you?"

"Find a forever love and be happy, no matter who it is. I love her dearly, but I see Tab going in a different direction once she graduates, and I know that will be hard. You're a good person, Cam, and the right one will come along. Be patient and love her dearly when she does."

Cam understood her mama's acceptance and her advice. She also felt that her time with Tab would be very limited. "I will, Mama."

"I know you feel like family always has to come first, but there will be a time when you need to take care of your heart and needs. Your sisters are growing up fast. They will survive and thrive on their own, so don't give up your happiness unnecessarily."

This was their goodbye conversation. Her sisters had all spent time with her the night before, but Cam had intentionally waited until last, knowing that she would have time with her at the hospital. She smiled at her mother. "I dreamed of the most pleasant memories last night, Mama. I know we shared so many good times together that it's hard to decide on the best."

"They were all the best to me. From the day you were born, until now, you've brought so much love and wonder into my life."

"You've always been my best friend, Mama. I'm going to miss you so much." Cam couldn't hold back her tears any longer. "It kills me to see you in so much pain, and there's not a damned thing I can do about it."

"The pain will be gone soon, and the medicine makes it more tolerable. It's the price of leaving one world for the next. I'm ready to go, Cam, but not ready to leave my beautiful girls and loving husband."

They fell silent for a short time. "There is something you can do," she finally said. "Call your dad in the morning before the girls go off to school. Ask him to bring them here to be with me when I leave. I don't want any of them sad that they missed out on that, but don't force them if that's not what they want. Especially Sandy. She's so young and tender."

Cam smiled. "She's probably the strongest one of the bunch of us, maybe not physically, but her heart is strong and she genuinely cares for others."

"She'll still need you more than the rest, simply because of her age, but I know you'll be there for her."

"Yes, ma'am, I will."

"I'm tired now, Cam. Please make that call in the morning."

"I will, Mama. I love you. Just rest. I'll be right here beside you."

"I love you too, Cam."

Cam watched her drift back to sleep, a beautiful smile on her face replacing the signs of pain she had been wearing for days. Her mama was relaxing, preparing for the journey home. She sat back and smiled.

A nurse stepped in. "Is there anything I can get you?"

"No, ma'am, but thank you," Cam replied.

At five, when she knew her dad would be up, Cam called home to give him her mama's last request. He and her sisters arrived at the hospital shortly after seven.

Camille was still resting peacefully when they entered the room. She woke when she felt their presence and smiled at them.

"I love you all," she whispered with a faint breath. Her eyes closed as she drifted back to sleep. Her heart rate began to decrease as they gathered around her bedside. With her children and her loving husband with her, Camille passed from this world in peace.

When the heart monitor showed a flat line, a nurse stepped into the room to silence it. "Stay as long as you need," she told Ronny. "I'm sorry for your loss."

He nodded as tears rolled down his cheeks.

Cam, who had stood by her side, bent down to kiss her forehead. "Goodbye, pretty lady." She stepped away from the bed to allow her sisters to say their final goodbyes. "We'll wait for you in the family room, Dad," she said as she hugged him, then took her sisters outside.

Even though they had prepared the best they could, the girls sat in stunned silence. Sandy was in Cam's lap, her arms wrapped around her neck. It seemed like hours since they'd left the room, but Ronny joined them only thirty minutes later.

He hugged them all and said, "Your mama is at peace. It's time for us to go home." He looked at Cam with weariness in his eyes. "Will you load the girls up? The truck is in the spot right beside you. I need to stop at the nurse's desk for a few minutes."

"We'll wait for you outside," Cam replied and led her sisters out of the hospital. It was a beautiful day, full of sunshine, and the birds were singing joyfully.

Perfect. Just how Mama would have wanted it.

"Buckle up buttercups," Cam told them as they filed into the two vehicles. Sandy and Wanda would normally have fought over the front seat of her Jeep, but Wanda silently climbed in behind Cam. She clearly sensed that Sandy needed Cam's closeness and watched as Sandy took Cam's hand as they waited for their dad to arrive.

"We don't have to go to school, do we?" she asked.

"No, sweetie, you don't," Cam assured her.

Cam looked into her rearview mirror to see their preacher talking with Ronny at the front door of the hospital. The preacher shook his hand and nodded in answer to a question from their father. She knew that her mama had insisted they put plans in place for her funeral, so when the time came they wouldn't have to fuss over small details.

Cam had helped her pick out her best Sunday dress and took it to the cleaners with her dad's best suit for the occasion. She knew if she opened up her mama's closet door, they would be there waiting to be worn, still protected in the plastic sleeves. There were calls to make and plans for what she and the girls would wear, but those could wait a few hours.

Cam followed her dad home and started a pot of coffee. "Will you take Willow out for me?" she asked Sandy.

Sandy nodded, having barely spoken a word since their mama had passed. Frowning, Cam watched her leave.

"Don't worry, she'll be okay," Ronny said.

"I know, Dad. What can I help you with?"

"You can start making some calls for me if you would? I've already asked the preacher to arrange for a funeral Friday. I'll call and confirm if you'll start calling friends and family." He handed her a list of names and phone numbers.

Cam took it, poured a cup of coffee, and walked out to the backyard to start. She sat on the bench under the pavilion in sight of Sandy and Willow playing together in the yard and called Tab.

"Mama's gone," she said when Tab answered. "Yes, just a little while ago. … Everyone's okay. Dad's arranging the services for Friday. … Yes, it would be great if you could come down. I'll let you know the details. Love you too. Call you later."

Cam made her way down the list. She called Bren at work and knew she would spread the word around LB's. Several of the ladies from the church volunteered to organize the wake, which would be held after the viewing Thursday night and would ensure the family had plenty of food, for themselves and guests who would drop in all week. Death was a busy occasion in the bayou.

Buster arrived to resume working on the house. When T gave him the news, the big, burly man broke down in tears. They walked hand in hand to the house they were building together and sat on the steps as they comforted one another.

Mama's only brother David was the last person on the list. He lived up in Lafayette and Cam hadn't seen him in years. She dialed the number, hoping it was still an active number. She sighed when after four rings, a man picked up. "Uncle David?"

"This is David. Who is this?"

"It's Cam. I'm calling to let you know Mama passed away this morning, and the service will be held Friday."

"I'm sorry, Cam, I didn't recognize your voice. You sound all grown-up. I talked with Camille right before Christmas and she knew she didn't have long. How is everyone doing?"

"Holding our own, I reckon." He seemed like such a stranger to Cam.

"Give everyone my love and tell Ronny I'll be down Thursday. Thanks, Cam."

"You're welcome. Safe travels."

Sandy walked over and sat beside Cam as she hung up.

"How ya doing, Squirt?"

"I feel numb. Is there something wrong with me?"

Cam hugged her close. "No, sweetie, I feel it too. No matter how hard we tried to prepare for Mama going to heaven, it still came as a shock when it happened."

"It's like my heart is empty."

"It's sad, but it will be happy again soon. Mama wouldn't want you to be sad for long. She's happy now, and not in pain."

"Happy that she's gone?" Sandy looked at her in confusion.

Cam selected her next words more carefully. "No, Mama didn't want to leave us behind, but it wasn't her choice to be called home. She was at peace and will no longer have to struggle with the pain of her illness."

"That makes sense. I miss her already."

"I know. I do too. She'll always be with us in our hearts and our memories."

"I won't forget her, will I?"

"No, baby, you won't. I'll make sure of that."

Sandy smiled up at her.

"I need some more coffee. Do you think you can help me make some pancakes?"

"Yeah, I think so, Cam."

"Let's go, then."

†

The next few days passed in a blur of activity as the family prepared for the services. The women from the church kept them well fed and helped the girls prepare their clothing for the funeral. Cam was relieved when Tab arrived Thursday morning, and she cried herself to sleep in Tab's arms after the viewing.

Cam dressed in black slacks and a steel-gray shirt Tab had bought for her, for the funeral. Tab was in a matching skirt and blouse. The girls wore their Sunday best, and Ronny wore a black suit with a white dress shirt. Tab helped him with the tie as his hands refused to cooperate.

"I tie my dad's all the time," she said after she was done. She kissed him on the cheek. "There, you look handsome. Mama would be proud." She regretted speaking the words as soon as they came out of her mouth as his eyes filled with tears. She pulled him into an embrace and held him tightly for several long minutes.

The long black limo from the funeral home arrived early to take them to the church for the services. Tab's hand slipped into Cam's as she gazed out the window. It was a beautiful morning, the sun shining brightly, without a cloud in the sky.

They walked into the church and found Camille's casket already in place. She looked beautiful, like she was sleeping peacefully as her family circled around her. Cam's uncle David arrived, and Cam walked outside for fresh air to allow others to say their goodbyes.

She and Tab were standing on the front lawn of the church when several familiar vehicles pulled into the lot. Tab held on to her arm as the doors opened and their teammates and coach climbed out.

Cam looked at Tab in shock. "Did you know they were coming?"

She smiled and nodded. "Once a team, always a family."

Coach was the first to arrive and place her arms around Cam. "I'm sorry for your loss. How are you and the family doing?"

"It's been a rough patch, Coach, but we're staying strong. Thanks for coming. I wasn't expecting this." Tears welled in her eyes as she hugged each of her teammates.

"I hope you don't mind, but we brought something for your mama." Ruth handed Cam a bright yellow softball with the slogan *Once a team, always a family* written on it, along with all their signatures in bright purple. "Mama meant a lot to all of us."

"Thank you so much. All of you, for being here, and this lovely gift. Would you place it beside Mama?" she asked Ruth.

Ruth smiled at her. "I'd love to."

The small group followed her inside, and they paid their respects to the family and circled around Camille's casket.

"She looks like she could wake up any minute," Liz whispered to Tab. "She looks beautiful."

The service was brief but well attended. Cam saw some people she hadn't seen in years fill the church and then join the procession to the cemetery. The staff from the funeral home worked quickly to arrange the flowers above the open crypt. The casket remained on the gurney for the short graveside service and was then placed inside the concrete vault. Visitors moved away from the crypt to give the family privacy, then followed them back home to celebrate Camille's passing.

Several women from the church had gone out to the house to deliver and prepare food for the arriving guests. Cam, Tab, and their friends walked out to the backyard to visit. They would pay their respects to the family and head back to Baton Rouge to prepare for a weekend series. Tab would stay the night and drive over early the next morning.

Cam took an opportunity to speak privately with Coach. "I can't tell you how special it was to have you all here with the family today. I know this is a hectic time for you all."

"It was a privilege to be here for you and the family, to honor your mama's passing. I do hope hearts will begin to mend and the family will continue to grow stronger together." Coach smiled and hugged her. "Bring those sisters of yours to a game soon. We miss hearing them in the stands and they are good luck charms for us."

Cam chuckled. "Please don't ever tell them that, or they'll get big heads."

"I promise, and my phone is always on if you need to talk. I'm proud of you, Cam."

"Thanks, Coach."

Cam and Tab walked out to the cars with them when it was time to leave.

"Come to a game soon," Parker implored as they hugged, then climbed into their vehicles.

"We'll see you soon," Cam promised. "Good luck this weekend."

She placed an arm around Tab's shoulder as they watched them drive away, then they walked back inside. Cam was glad when the crowd started to thin out, and only two ladies from the church remained to put away the food.

"Thank you all for your wonderful gifts of food and support to the family this week. You made a difficult time much easier for us all," Cam told them as they prepared to leave.

"Camille was a very special woman and has provided us with so much comfort in her short life. It was a pleasure being here for you all, and I hope you'll call on us if you need anything," one of the women said.

"We will," Cam assured her, and Ronny walked them out to their cars.

The girls were quick to change into comfortable clothes, and Ronny came back into the house tugging the tie from around his neck.

"If everyone is good here, Tab and I are going across to the camp to change clothes."

Ronny nodded. "Yes, honey, I think we just all need to relax."

"We will come back for some leftovers around six. Is that okay?"

"That sounds perfect. See you soon."

†

When they arrived at the camp, Cam looked at Tab. "I need a nap."

"You didn't sleep very well last night. Mind if I join you?"

"I was hoping you would." Cam took her hand and led her to the bedroom.

They undressed and slipped beneath the covers, and Cam reached for Tab who rolled onto her side to tuck her head into Cam's shoulder.

"I love you, Tab."

"Love you too, Cam."

CHAPTER TWELVE

Cam kept her promise, and three weeks after the funeral, she took Sandy and Wanda to a ball game. It was difficult to sit in the stands when her heart was aching to be out in the field. Several of the fans recognized her, gave their condolences on her mama's passing, and said they hoped she'd be back to playing ball soon. Cam just smiled and thanked them for their comfort.

They cheered wildly as Tab and the team destroyed the Georgia Bulldogs. Tab played well and had taken up Cam's routine of kissing the charm she wore around her neck prior to each at bat. It seemed to help as she went three for four at the plate. Parker played well at shortstop, but there were many plays Cam knew she could have made, if she'd only been on the field.

She almost felt sorry for the bruises and sore spots she was sure she inflicted upon her sisters as she lunged and stretched to make plays from the bleacher. Fortunately, they both just laughed and teased her.

After the game, Coach walked up to them. "It's good to see y'all."

"Thanks, Coach. It's full-swing mudbug season, but we decided to take a day off to see you chomp on some Bulldogs."

"I'm glad you did. You look good, Cam. I hope you can join us for some other games this season, and maybe the conference tournament."

"We'll see how things go." She waited for Tab to shower, and then they went to dinner.

"I'm glad you all could come for the game. You sure you can't stay the night?"

"We'd love too, but we promised Dad we'd be back late tonight to help harvest the mudbugs in the morning," Cam explained. "The folks in town eat them faster than we can catch them and we've tripled our pots this year."

"Just remember to save a batch for us. Ruth and Liz have already informed me we're coming down for a visit in three weeks when we have an off date."

Cam smiled. "Liz did mention that earlier. We'll be ready. Come as soon as you can, and we'll make a weekend of it."

Sandy perked up. "The fish are hitting again. Maybe you could fish with me."

"I bet you could even talk Ruth into it too," Cam said.

"That would be awesome." Sandy took another bite.

When they finished eating, Sandy and Wanda climbed into the Jeep while Cam chatted with Tab.

"I wish I could stay, but it's been crazy busy."

"I understand. It was good to see y'all even for a short visit."

"Once the mudbugs slow down, I'll see if I can sneak away during the week, when the girls are in school. It's almost impossible to tell them no when it's the weekend."

Tab laughed. "It's okay. Call to let me know you made it home okay?"

"It may be late."

"That's fine. I'll sleep better once I hear from you."

Cam pulled her into a hug and kissed her softly. "I love you. See you soon."

"Love you more," Tab said.

She watched Cam climb into the Jeep and pull away, three hands waving furiously at her as they disappeared into the night.

†

Later that spring, Ronny pulled the girls together for a meeting. He and Cam explained to them the importance of incorporating and the effect it would have on their futures. The businesses were doing well, and T would graduate in a couple of months and could help more with some of the projects. Karen and Wanda would be right behind her in a couple of years. Karen and Jeff, Buster's younger brother, were dating, and it looked like another year and more wedding bells might be ringing. Wanda had already enrolled in a few online college courses for her junior year so she could get a head start on attending college. Life was good on the homestead.

After they finished the meeting, Cam stayed to talk with her dad. "I was wondering if you'd consider a proposition."

"I'm listening."

"Tab will graduate next year and move on to law school in North Carolina. If Coach can get me back on scholarship next fall, how would you feel if I went back for one more shot at Oklahoma City? I could take a business course or two to make me eligible to play. After that, I'd be a hundred percent into the Gator Girlz."

"Considering all you have sacrificed for the family, there's no way I could say no to you, Cam. T graduating will be a big help, so I think we can hold things together for another year of college. You're going down for the tournament this weekend, aren't you?"

"Yes, sir. I'd like to talk to Coach but waited until I could run it past you."

"Good. Let me know what she thinks. We can cook like crazy this summer and build up some stock. The girls and I can handle the rest. Maybe Buster or Jeff can help me out during gator season too."

"I'll come home on the weekends for that. We can run two boats and fill the tags quicker."

"Great idea, Madam President." He smiled.

†

When she drove to the tournament later that week, she shared her idea with Tab, who was ecstatic about the possibility of her return.

"That would be great on so many levels, Cam. When do you plan on talking to Coach?"

"In about a half hour. I have a meeting set up with her at seven, then I thought we could grab a late dinner."

"Fantastic, but my treat, okay?" Tab insisted.

"I won't complain," Cam agreed.

Cam paced nervously until it was time to go for her meeting with Coach. When she walked down the hall to her hotel room, the light was on and Cam knocked on the door.

Coach opened it and smiled as Cam stepped into her room. "Come on in and have a seat." She walked over to sit beside Cam on the couch "You look great. How have you been?"

"Pretty good. I need to ask something before I lose my nerve. Would it be possible for me to get my scholarship back for one more year? I'd like to return next fall for one more shot at OKC and to be here with Tab for her final year. Then I need to go home to run the family business."

Coach surprised her by jumping out of her chair and grabbing her. "I was hoping you'd asked for a meeting to discuss coming back. I'll move heaven and earth if that's what it takes to get you back in school, Cam. You leave everything for me to arrange, and I'll be in touch to let you know what the fall schedule will look like."

"I'd like to focus on a few business classes. Nothing heavy, just enough to make me eligible to play."

"Will you be available for summer camps?"

"Yes, ma'am. I plan to start working out, and help with coaching Wanda's high school team, to get back in playing shape."

"You look better than ever, Cam."

"Physically, yes, but it's been forever since I picked up a bat."

"You're a natural. The swing will still be there, maybe even better."

"Only time will tell." Cam grinned. "Thank you for this opportunity."

Coach nodded with tears in her eyes. "One last thing."

"What's that?"

"Will you bring Sandy and Wanda to camps with you this summer?"

Cam burst out laughing. "As if I could get away and leave them home. Trust me, their bags will be packed as soon as I know dates."

"Great, I'll save them both spots."

Cam hugged her tightly. "Thanks, Coach."

"Thank you, Cam. I'll see you at the games tomorrow."

"Good night. Hey, is it okay to share with Ruth and Liz?"

"Yes. But let me announce it to the rest of the team after the tournament. I want to keep them focused."

"You got it."

†

Cam broke the news to her friends over dinner, and they were excited that she'd be rejoining the team.

"I wish I had another year of eligibility left," Liz groaned.

"I do too, Liz." Cam smiled at her. "With only one shot left, I've got to do everything I can to make it happen for us."

"Mind you, I don't want you to be injured, but could you fake an injury to get a medical–redshirt year?" Ruth asked.

"I think we're already beyond that window," Liz replied. "You can bet we'll be in OKC to support y'all if you make it, though."

"Just as I hope to be this year," Cam replied.

"Parker will be excited at the news." Ruth laughed. "She hates playing shortstop."

"That's a relief. I worried she'd be offended."

"Not in the least, and we will all appreciate your power at the plate. Coach and I have been recruiting some bigger bats across the state for next year. Their power would complement yours well," Ruth added.

"I've got my work cut out for me this summer, then, helping Dad get stocked up and getting back into playing shape."

"Will you be coming to the summer camps?" Liz asked.

"Coach has already asked and has spots saved for Wanda and Sandy too. Oh. Speaking of Sandy, she's planning a fishing date with you and Tab when you come down for a boil," she told Ruth.

Ruth grinned. "Tell Squirt I'll be looking forward to it."

†

Ronny surprised them by bringing Sandy and Wanda down for the tournament, and they all cheered for the Tigers, who finished in third place. The players were excited to hear that Cam would be rejoining the team, which softened the

232

blow when they learned they hadn't made the cut for the Regionals. But Coach rallied their spirits.

"We'll just have to work even harder next year. Cam will be back to play shortstop, and we have some really strong recruits coming in next fall."

"Hallelujah, Cam, you have made my day. I am not half the shortstop you are, but I'll gladly take over for Liz at first," Parker said.

"That's not a bad option," Coach said. "Let's see how the summer and fall go."

†

Later that day, Sandy rode home with Cam, while Wanda drove her dad home. She received her license the previous year but didn't spend a lot of time driving. But with Cam going back to the school in the fall, Ronny needed all hands-on deck, so Wanda practiced driving in the big city. After they cleared the I-10 Bridge leaving Baton Rouge, it was smooth sailing, but Cam guessed that Wanda had held her breath until they had gotten across.

She smiled over at her baby sister. "I hope you're ready for a long hard summer."

"Right beside ya, Cam." Sandy grinned back at her.

ABOUT THE AUTHOR

ALI SPOONER

Ali Spooner, a native of Florida, is currently living and working in Pensacola, Florida. As an "indie" author, Ali has been writing for many years as a hobby, and with the assistance of the Affinity team has taken her love of storytelling to a new level.

Ali's characters range from cowgirls and psychics, to a healthy dose of supernatural beings. She has written stand-alone titles and series. Ali is an avid reader, and her other hobbies include photography, outdoor activities, and watching college sports.

OTHER AFFINITY BOOKS

<u>The Tempest</u> by JM Dragon
Doctor Alana Cameron has dedicated her life to working on the family legacy, a transportation device which will change the world for everyone, called Tempest. Super soldier, Major Denise Trantor, who loyally defends Earth in any way possible finds herself drawn into the Tempest program. Because of her military training, emotional bonding is not in her remit although she finds herself inexplicably drawn to Alana.

<u>Trusting Hearts</u> by Samantha Hicks
When successful advertising executive Carrie-Ann Stedman is tasked to train a new hire, she is reluctant. She has never forgiven Holly Fletcher, the newbie, for stealing an important client away from her. Holly doesn't know what

Carrie's problem with her is. When the two are thrown together can they build a working relationship with business getting in the way of the growing attraction between them?

<u>Free to Love</u> by Ali Spooner and Annette Mori
Captain Hillary Blythe loves sailing the ocean. Her journeys along the Atlantic Coast and Caribbean to deliver goods contain many adventures. When she brings a small group of rescued Africans to the Methodist mission on Antigua, challenges to deeply ingrained beliefs arise when she is drawn to one of the women—Kia.. Will Kia and Elizabeth be free to love among the harsh laws of the land and Elizabeth's struggles with her faith?

<u>Diamond Dreams</u> by Ali Spooner
Cameron St. Angelo dreams of playing softball in the College World Series. Earning a scholarship to play ball for her beloved LSU brings Cam one-step closer to achieving this dream. When Cam arrives on campus, she joins a family of women who share her love of the sport, and she realizes there is room in her life for another love.

<u>Unconventional Lovers</u> by Annette Mori
Bri and Siera are young women with huge hearts and strong wills; they want nothing more than to find a peaceful and secure space to be themselves. But the world is a harsh place for anyone who is different. Bri's Aunt Olivia is a vet who channels her emotions into her work and her love of Bri. Siera has her Aunt Deb who adores her. Despite their

individual battles against hurt, prejudice and rejection, can these four women find love against the odds?

<u>Say You Won't Go</u> by JM Dragon & Erin O'Reilly
Logan Perry spent part of an inheritance traveling to various states, unconsciously looking for something to focus her life on. Taryn Donovan has no self-esteem and hates the waitressing job that barely keeps her in food. Can an unexpected weekend encounter turn out to be something more fulfilling? Find out in this sexually charged romance.

<u>Playing with Matches</u> by Lacey Schmidt
Dr Augusta Stuart has devoted her adult life to supporting the mental health of disadvantaged children and moves to a new clinic in San Antonio. Her friend sets her up on a date with Callia Alexana. Prickly debates are somehow as unexpectedly fascinating as playing with matches, and Gus is forced to consider what preconceptions she is willing to burn to find true love.

<u>Changing Perspectives</u> by Jen Silver
Art director, Dani Barker, lives life on the edge and finance director Camila Callaghan thinks it's necessary to stay in the closet to maintain her position. When Dani and Camila meet, they both sense an attraction, A change of perspective for both women is needed if they are to act on it.

<u>Death is Only the Beginning</u> by JM Dragon
What would you do if you were in a fatal accident with a stranger and ended up in heaven with them? Only to find out it wasn't an accident, it was murder. Follow the ghostly adventures of these two acrimonious strangers, who help two women find love and find closure for their predicament.

<u>For the Love of a Woman</u> by S. Anne Gardner
Enter a world where oil is supreme, passion rules reason and there is always the threat of civil war. In this jungle of power Raisa Andieta resides as one of its masters. Her only desire is to rule it alone. Carolyn Stenbeck is just trying to keep her marriage together. Her only desire is to be able to escape and never look back. When Raisa and Carolyn meet, it is like fuel and fire…a storm is brewing. Civil War is in the air, and passion like the coming storm begins to erupt.

<u>The Bee Charmer</u> by Ali Spooner
After the death of her father, Nat St. Croix needs to decide on which direction her life should take. Does she continue her life alone, as a trapper and trader, or does she start over and try to fit into a town surrounded by strangers? Will the call of the wild and all that is familiar win out, or will the call of love capture Nat's heart?

Affinity
Rainbow Publications

eBooks, Print, Free eBooks

Visit our website for more publications available online.

www.affinityrainbowpublications.com

Published by Affinity Rainbow Publications
A Division of Affinity eBook Press NZ LTD
Canterbury, New Zealand

Registered Company 2517228